The Cut

Born in Dudley in 1973, Anthony Cartwright is the author of four previous novels, published by Serpent's Tail, most recently *Iron Towns* (2016), which was praised in both the *Guardian* ('Cartwright achieves something bold in *Iron Towns*: a fictional enactment of communal identity and shared culture... expert, restrained and skilful') and the *Daily Mail* (A gritty, moving elegy for an abandoned, once-thriving section of society'). His novels have been shortlisted for various literary awards, including the Commonwealth Writers' Prize and the Gordon Burn Prize, and *Heartland* was adapted for BBC Radio 4's *Book at Bedtime*. Anthony has also published a collaborative novel with Gian Luca Favetto, *Il giorno perduto* (The Lost Day), released in Italy in 2015. He lives in London with his wife and son.

MEIKE ZIERVOGEL
PEIRENE PRESS

The result of the EU referendum shocked me. I realized that I had been living in one part of a divided country. What fears – and what hopes – drove my fellow citizens to vote for Brexit? I commissioned Anthony Cartwright to build a fictional bridge between the two Britains that have opposed each other since the referendum day.

First published in 2017 by Peirene Press
17 Cheverton Road
London N19 3BB
www.peirenepress.com

ISBN 978-1-908670-40-3

Designed by Sacha Davison Lunt
Photographic image by Steven Roe/EyeEm
Typeset by Tetragon, London
Printed and bound by T J International, Padstow, Cornwall

ANTHONY CARTWRIGHT

Peirene

The Cut

After

The young woman runs burning along the side of the marketplace, down the High Street, away from the fountain. Away from the fountain and the cool, litter-strewn water. She is tall, long-legged. Her hair is ablaze and flames spit from an unravelling scarf towards the motley crowd of people who give chase. Someone is screaming, but it is not the woman. She breathes fire. There is the slap of cheap sandals on the pavement behind her.

'Stop her,' someone shouts. 'Just fucking stop her.'

A man runs at the edge of the crowd, a camera on his shoulder, filming, does not stop the running woman. The procession ripples across shop windows and puddles from the earlier rain.

Then she falls, arms and legs and flames, and the men and women and kids crowd around her, with their heads bowed, their arms across their faces against the smell of burning hair, burning flesh. The scarf melts into the young woman's face. The people roll her on the ground, with some sense of what to do. What to do if a woman comes running through the market on a Friday afternoon in the middle of England with her head on fire.

Cairo is hit from behind and keels forward so that he watches this side on, his head on the slabs, through fire and smoke, heat, the world watery in his eyes, and jagged and half-formed. There are people running. He feels the blows as they strike him, watches through their arms and legs.

A woman on her mobility scooter, an outrider of the chase, takes a blanket from her lap. The people wrap the burning woman in this and a lad's red tracksuit top. The clothes begin to stick to her. And the people bicker about whether they are doing the right thing. They bend on either side of the fallen woman, rock her gently. Others gather with phones raised and aimed in witness. There are sirens now. One of the attendant men stands, stumbles and coughs, heaves into the gutter and sits down on the kerb, the cuffs of a torn work shirt rolled back and his burnt hands held out in front of him.

The woman on the mobility scooter beckons towards the man with the camera on his shoulder, who continues to film, and he approaches her, still filming. She pulls herself up, looks into the camera, which sees her soft, round English face twist behind her glasses, and she spits hard at the lens.

The taste of ash, burnt flesh.

There is a blackened stump in his mouth. And darkness, then light, darkness then light, in the pattern of flames against a dark hillside, the pattern of lights across a dark plain under hills.

To begin again, the day, his life, to begin.

The day begins with rain and Cairo curses it, wills it to stop. He holds his ankle support in his hand and looks at the trees through the bedroom window, the rain-dashed glass. Even with the weather this morning and a stiffness in his legs, he feels a sense of pulling through. He was always a stayer. When he phoned Jamie Iqbal the man had not said no.

'You must be forty-five years old, Cairo. I don't think I have ever heard anything like this in my life,' Jamie said to him.

They had barely spoken for – what? – ten years. Except for that one night at the restaurant with Grace. Cairo tries not to think about that.

'Thirty-eight. I'm thirty-eight,' he said to Jamie.

He has not been thirty-eight for a good while, but forty-five is taking the piss. He knows they change names, ages, everything – you become someone new – at Jamie Iqbal's nights. It's not as if he wants his licence back. He tells himself he is not a fool, wonders whether in the telling there is some foolishness he cannot fathom.

He moves through the quiet rooms, the sound of a family asleep. Through the half-open bedroom door he sees the cot, the mobile that he sat up late to put together, zoo animals suspended in morning light. He steps into the room, aware of the creak of the floorboards, the sagging house. The boy's fists are curled tight, his face serious in sleep, the flicker of his eyes beneath thin lids. A beautiful, dreaming boy, strong-looking, solid and real. Not like the other child in his, Cairo's, head, unformed, spectral.

His daughter stirs in the bed, turns, her mouth open and her shoulders bare, still asleep, and Cairo steps backwards, out of the door, and stands there on the landing to wait and see if he has woken them, and wonders if he can do anything else right now except let them sleep a little longer.

If the fight is to take place it will be in Birmingham, not far from the Villa, at an abandoned furniture showroom by the Perry Barr dogs, now that Jamie has closed the restaurant. Cairo takes it as a good omen, enjoyed fighting in Birmingham as a kid. This new place has white-collar bouts and unlicensed meetings on the first Friday of the month. How white-collar boxing differs from that of his own people Cairo is not sure. He is blue collar. He is possibly no collar. This is something he would like to say to Jamie, something he would have liked to have said to Grace had things been different. She would've laughed. He woke thinking he heard a baby cry out, and perhaps it was Zach, and Stacey-Ann comforted him in the time it took Cairo to wake, silence in the house when he sat up and listened, and perhaps it was that other baby calling out from somewhere else.

Carefully he walks down the stairs. One foot in front of the other is how to do it.

'You said you thought I could still handle meself.'

'Thass a figure of speech, Cairo. Jesus.'

'Just come and have a look. See what yer think,' he said.

'I cor believe I'm bloody listenin to yer.'

'You know yer can trust me, Jay. You know that much.'

'How many years is it, Cairo, how many?'

'Honest to God.'

'How's yer ode mon?' Jamie's voice softened.

'Older.'

'Jesus, it's me that wants their head lookin at, not yow.'

'You know yer can trust me, Jay. Just come and have a look.'

And that's how they'd left it, had exchanged texts. Before Cairo smashed up his phone, that is. Jamie will come, Cairo knows it. It is this thought now that gets him up the hill, early mornings, late nights if he can, depending on work and his aching bones.

From the kitchen window he watches the fox go over the back fence with a scrabble of claws in the grey light. Maybe he didn't hear a baby but instead the fox in the night. There are no ghosts, he tells himself, doubts this even as he thinks it.

Cairo pulls back the net curtain, lets his finger pattern the condensation. He drinks slowly from his water bottle, the taste of old gyms somewhere in it. Blood in water. There is a whole history of men who got beaten up, knocked senseless, in order to pay the rent, put food on the table, one of the many histories buried in the hill. He tells himself he is part of a proud Dudley tradition.

A face looms from the dark and then is gone, his face, it was his face. But how could that be? There are voices that come through the permanent night, soothing and calm, though she doesn't know what they say. She lies, suspended, is not sure where her body might be, nor the body that grows inside her own, swimming in the dark, no sense of the shore, no sense of the surface, but it is calm and there is no pain. She drifts, thinks of tiny creatures fixed in amber for thousands of years.

Grace swims in the morning, when she should've been packing her bags, in the arboreal light of the Ladies' Pond. She loves the word arboreal, loves this place, and turns to watch the clouds through the trees, moves into a cool, dark channel in shadow, near the bank, then out again into sunlight. She has one bag packed, of course, but no passport or papers inside it. No euros or forints or dinar wrapped carefully in envelopes. She remembers she must show Zara where these are, in the small safe in the corner of the studio, and that she must give her the codes. She will not return there after this morning. She wants a clean break.

Zara and the crew will be flying to Budapest, then onwards in jeeps from there, towards the border, always this crossing of borders, real or imagined. The idea is to return to the towns and villages they'd filmed before, in their first film, the one that won the award and has kept them in work these last few years, villages in corners of the Balkans. They told a story of how people left and how new people came, recorded daily life going about its business, women making burek filmed through open windows, old men herding goats, timeless but fractured somehow. Sometimes they got people to talk: 'We came here when we had to leave our old homes.' They told stories of movement and place and great violence. That she, Grace, found the pictures so beautiful, the stillness of the images, the depth of the colours, the incongruity of what the words described when anyone spoke, and that other people felt the same, appals her now, makes her feel ashamed. This is not a feeling she has ever considered before: shame. Like something from a distant century, a forgotten civilization, something talked about in films of faraway places.

The sun makes a path of light across the surface of the pond. Grace suddenly sees herself again as a girl at the end of the lane near her grandparents' house, where she'd go after school to drink cocoa or cordial. Cocoa and cordial: two things and words of which her grandmother was fond. Her grandmother who also had swum here in the pond. And as a young woman she had swum in the Thames, of course, called it the Isis, as Grace had, and her mother had too. And as a young girl her grandmother swam in the Shannon, daughter of Empire. They have a tea set in the attic at home, come all the way from India in a trunk, the tiniest spidery cracks in the china.

But first Grace has to finish her current project, one way or the other, will go back today, last images, not to the middle of Europe but to the middle of England. And then she'll see.

She must leave the water. She will tell Zara and Andrew this morning. She will wish them luck, and tell them she is leaving, she is making her own film in Dudley after all, which they know about and have dismissed, smiled indulgently at the thought of a film about England, the England she has filmed. Although to be fair they have lent her equipment, offered her Franco for a few days' work when they are not using him. She could tell Zara about the baby too. Grace has told no one yet. She feels the brush of feathery wings within her. New life. It is still too early to feel anything like that for real, surely, her mind playing tricks on her. But then what does she know about it all?

Of course she is leaving them in a mess, and she fears she has become exactly that: a person who leaves a mess behind and then moves on. Other people will clear up. And perhaps she has always been such a person. Perhaps they all have. That was the gist of what Cairo had said, after all.

She tries to roll onto her back for one last loop of the pond and feels dizzy and rights herself, like a ship with shifting ballast, and she wonders where that image could have come from, her own life far from the sea. Her dad used to claim a pirate heritage, ancestors who hoarded treasure in Cornish caves. As a girl she loved this idea, would hop between fallen branches on the Heath wielding her cutlass at the frothing waves.

She feels OK doing a steady front crawl, on an even keel. There is a woman ahead of her, wearing a thick swimming hat that does not fit her head and looking serene all the same. She should suggest that her mother start swimming again. Her mother in fact will be the only one to feel unambiguously relieved about her, Grace, not catching that flight to Budapest, Grace herself included.

'Thank God for that,' her mother will almost certainly say.

Grace sees herself already, ten minutes, half an hour, an hour hence. Drying herself with her thin towel, a deliberate nod to her grandmother's disdain for any kind of luxury, her mother's too, and pulling her clothes on too quickly, hurrying down the hill to Gospel Oak and buying a coffee on the way, self-consciously asking for decaff, the innumerable greys of the view across London, the patterns of a pigeon's wing, the light and shade of the city, something that is part of her, she supposes, and she has only thought about since watching the interviews back time and again, since the conversations, what else to call them, the encounters. And then, later, the confrontation.

'The idea that the land and the people are indivisible,' was something Cairo had said. Indivisible: a word he probably didn't use very often.

'I'm not coming with you,' she will say this morning to Zara and Andrew, over the sound of the traffic and the trains, with the light slanting through the studio. It bothers her that her hair will still be wet when she says this, and it bothers her that this bothers her.

Before

And on the day on which they met there had been similar weather, early rain and then bright, with high clouds moving fast in the wind, a chill to it, but warm enough in the sun. She met him in this shifting light, his head held high and smiling, in his work clothes, covered in a film of dust. He said later that the clouds were called the Severn Jacks, for the way they moved up the river, but she could find no reference to this, asked a couple of the older people she spoke to and they looked back at her blankly, as with so many of the questions she asked, the river was miles away after all. And she scolded herself that she did not have the right questions, that what she was doing was all in her own voice, not theirs.

'Be quiet, listen, let people speak,' was her mother's one piece of advice about interviews, maybe for life itself. 'Easier said than done,' she would always add. Her mother had her own doubts about getting people to say things on the radio that they might later regret, although she'd made a career of it. When Grace thought about it later, the river, the clouds, it made her wonder quite how much else Cairo had made up, how much it was his imagination that shifted and coloured what he said to her, like the movement of the sky itself. That his was a town, a whole country, of shifting, magical thinking was something that came to her much later as well.

That first morning she still believed in questions and answers.

Earlier in the morning she had tried to film interviews near the bottom of the High Street, and no one wanted to talk to her, but instead veered away if she approached, as if she might be asking a question to which they did not know the answer. She felt exposed here, even in a sheltered spot in the sun, across from the coloured market awnings and the football statue, of a giant man aiming a football down the hill, people passing by. A man wearing a brown cardigan over baggy mosque robes nodded and looked towards her but turned away, held a flower-patterned shopping bag in each hand as if to balance himself. The woman with the hooped earrings and red lipstick, wearing a tracksuit and seventy years old at least, *if she was a day*, to think of a phrase her dad might have once used, a woman who, Grace felt, was certain to want to speak to her, and whom she had even begun talking to before the woman stopped her with a thick, raised hand and said, 'Yow ay selling me nothing, am yer?'

'No, I just want to ask you something.'

'Thass what they all say,' and she had waddled on her way towards the bus station.

There were very thin young women who smoked over pushchair hoods and narrowed their eyes through the smoke at her. She felt like there was some kind of invisible veil between her and these people. *These people.* And this is how it began, she supposed, prejudice on the scale of a whole country. It was why she had come here, to say something about this. She did not even try to speak to the young women.

Then they came around the corner. She did not see Cairo first, that is she did not differentiate between the scrum of men, seven or eight of them but seeming more somehow, filling the street, who walked, laughing and loud, up the hill towards her, people's heads turning as they went. She saw them as a bobbing, swaggering whole. She was struck by the state of their work clothes, ragged and dirty like something from an engraving of Victorian squalor except in bright, cheap football colours and paint-splattered overalls, phones to their ears.

The younger men – boys, she supposed, some of them – played around in front of the camera. She cannot remember even approaching them, they came to her. The older men held back, Cairo was one of them, and she noticed him then, while the younger lads messed about in front of her. She asked them about the referendum, whether they would vote.

'Fuck that, man,' said one of the younger boys who now congregated before her, did not wear work clothes.

He sat with a bike askew beneath him and a cap askew on his head, chewing on a drinking straw, said something that she didn't catch to the other boys, who all laughed and looked at her. There was a sudden sense of menace. But when she watched the footage back it seemed much more innocent, reminded her of old pop bands mugging for the camera, like the Beatles' home-video tapes. Or even, regarding the older men who stood apart here, like men they had filmed once in Priština, men who had been soldiers and felt they had nothing left to prove to anyone at all, least of all a British film crew.

Cairo spoke across the group of posturing boys.

'Cut that out,' he said, looking at the boy in the cap.

'What?'

'You know what.'

The boy moved, sucked his teeth, but after a moment looked down.

'Come,' the boy said to the others, and walked with his legs either side of his bike away from them.

The younger boys began to straggle away, the energy sagged for a moment. She remembered the urge to thank him, this man with blue eyes, speckled with dust, and stopped herself. And she thought much later, how pathetic, to fall for something so simple, so primitive, really, his urge to protect her, or at least go through the motions of this, her willingness to be protected. This is later, when she was tearing herself apart. At the time she was grateful.

'I'll speak to yer, yeah. Come on,' is what he said.

And she was grateful for this too. This was the interview that played on and off for months, shared on Twitter and repeated on news cycles, the one she sold, which gave her enough money to actually employ Franco as a cameraman for a couple of days and set about making the film, which interested funders, which set the whole thing in motion, one small piece of the collage of images and things said that had come to define the vote on screens in the weeks both before and after it happened.

'We've had enough,' is what he said, with the sun on the footballer and the church and the castle behind him and the soft shadow of the buildings and his face dusted with some unknown material, which he would no doubt breathe in and whatever it was would be there in his lungs, burning through the years, the dust speckling his handsome face, his cheekbones, and his eyes shining out from the dust, daring you to keep looking, challenging you, as he stared into the camera and was not meant to, spoke directly to the people on the other side of the screen, mocking slightly, a smile not far from his lips, but deadly serious. 'We've had enough,' and he went on, and sometimes on television they put subtitles under his words, translated into his own language, and sometimes they did not. But there he was, playing on some endless loop, making sense, not making sense at all, and she knew, the moment he looked at the camera and started talking, knew it the moment he said, 'I'll speak to yer, yeah. Come on,' that something shifted inside her. And she could tell herself now that this was all in retrospect, that she was creating a story that was not there, a kind of bitter nostalgia taking hold of her, and possibly bitter nostalgia was a kind of answer to the question she should've been posing all along, but she knew that she was not that cynical. That all these feelings had been real.

'Cairo, we'll see yer up there, mate,' one of the other men, the darker, older one, the one who had kept out of the way of the camera, and whom she wanted to film because of that, called over to him, another man with a face of shadows and light. Cairo raised his hand, half turned, waved as if to dismiss them. She saw the small, dark man swear into his moustache.

'I won't keep you, Cairo, but thanks for your time.' She used his name straight away, wanted to ask him about it.

'Doh worry about them. We finished some work early today. They'm happy to get paid. We'm going for a drink to celebrate. Some money in their pockets. For a bit, any road.'

'What do you do?' she said, and pointed to the disclaimer form for him to sign after she'd explained what she was doing, not sure herself, testing the waters, trying to get the voices of ordinary people, conscious of saying ordinary people and all that might mean, on the way they might vote, and why.

'Clean up industrial sites, you know, tatting basically. You know what that is?' He smiled like it was a joke. 'We dig ditches and knock down old walls. Pick up bits of scrap for the gaffer.'

'There's a lot to clean up, from what I can see.'

'The place is a mess, is what you mean.'

'No, I didn't mean.'

But of course she did, in a way, because from the train window that morning she had looked at an expanse of rubble as they came out of Birmingham, a motorway flyover somewhere, the curve of iron bridges creating a mesh that reflected back in the canal water. It struck her that the place was best approached by water, along the narrow canals, from out of the green hills or through canyons of blackened brick. It was a cliché, not the whole story at all, like the stares of those young women, like the stares of those young men, but it was part of the story, no doubt.

He smiled. 'Keeping us in work, any road. What else am yer filming?'

The truth was that she didn't know, but she was on to something, wasn't sure what to say. She needed him to be interested in it.

'I'm back and forth for a few weeks,' she said, and was not sure if this was a lie or she was wishing it into being. 'They say the UKIP bus will be here at some point, it's coming here, I mean right here, to the marketplace, I think. Farage, you know.'

'I'll give that a miss.' He smiled, gentler than she imagined.

'I thought he might interest you, given what you've said.' This sense of wanting to pick away at something, that there was something more to what he was trying to

23

say. Only a few minutes ago she attempted to hide her surprise at how articulate he had been with his answers to her. He spoke of the weight of the past on the present, a sense of betrayal, of something undone, of retribution on some grand, futile scale.

'Oh no, don't get me wrong. I doh want nothing to do with him, nor any of em to be honest. We've had enough of folks like that and all. I cor speak for everybody here, of course. Anyway.'

He made a motion to leave. She wanted more, wanted to dig deeper.

She asked him about immigration. He looked at her. She felt she had struck some kind of nerve.

'I've told you what I think, that people have had enough of a lot of things.'

'But obviously you live in a place where there has been a lot of immigration.'

'All you people want to say is that it's about immigration. That we'm all racist. That we'm all stupid. You doh wanna hear that it's more complicated than that. It lets all of you lot off the hook. Never considered the problem might be you.'

You people, is what struck her. That and the anger that flickered for a moment in his eyes, her own anger ignited briefly. *You people*, these judgements. She was not so blind to herself to realize it might have been her own prejudice reflected back at her. *You people. These people.*

'Can I ask what you mean by "you people"?'

'On the telly, and that, like you can see everybody else's faults but your own.'

It seemed suddenly as if he would rather be anywhere else, he looked away and then back at her. 'I'm sorry, love. I don't know you. I don't mean to be rude. I shouldn't have stopped. Like I say, I think people here have had enough of a lot of things.'

'No, what you were saying was interesting.' She understood as she said this that she did so to placate him, to keep him talking, but to barb him too. *I'm sorry, love* irritated her. She wondered if her courtesy might flare the rage in him, but then what did she know of men like him? 'I'd like to understand more of what you meant, and about what you said about here, the experiences of this town, your own experiences.'

He shook his head as if surfacing from water.

'I don't think so,' he said.

There was an awkward moment. She held out her hand for him to shake. He looked uncertain what to do, wiped his hands against his torn blue sweatshirt.

He had already turned to walk away when he said, 'Listen, if you need any help,' motioned for the pen and scribbled a number on the edge of the form, passed her the paper in a hurry, as if before he changed his mind. 'Look, what I mean is, I could probably show you some places.'

'I'm sure you could, Cairo.' There she went, using his name again, a Gypsy name, could be, some history to it, some weight, flirting with him, trying to make a joke, put him at some sort of ease, knowing that she needed a way in. She looked at his hands as he passed her the slip of paper.

'Anyway,' he said.

'That's kind of you, really nice of you.'

He was already walking away.

'I'll give you a missed call and you'll have my number.' She started jabbing at her phone, a little bit too quickly perhaps. 'Grace,' she said, 'my name's Grace Trevithick.' She had already told him her name. She had a card that she could have given him, did not want to. He did not look like a man who dealt in business cards.

'It was very nice to meet you, Grace,' is what he said, formal all of a sudden, a man out of time in his torn work clothes, walking off up the High Street. She watched him go, she remembered, had wondered if he would turn to look back.

He didn't.

After

That boy from Lupin Road is ahead of him. Again.
Cairo pulls himself up the hill, conscious of his ankle as
he turns. His ankle, his hip, his knees. It is not his head
that anyone should be worried about. It never has been
his head, not really, although you let people hit you in
it for a living you might expect some sort of trouble.
No, the only issue he has ever had is being too clever
for his own good.

Summer is fading now, the rain coming down.

He looks at the soles of the boy's trainers as he strides
up St John's Road. His feet barely touch the ground. His
ankles and calves are slender. His broad back is heading away up the hill. Cairo is sure that he's wearing a
Saracen's Head club top, or Saracens now, as they must
call it, the name was changed a while ago. The red top is
one reason he wants to get nearer to the boy. That, and
to prove to himself that he's still got it in him, chasing
down someone half his age. Up the hill. Eating the yards,
the miles. Yet there is no sense of this being hard work

for the kid. While Cairo, on the other hand, is knackered. A weariness in his bones that he tells himself he can outrun, and some mornings truly believes.

They attack the steepest part of the hill. The boy turns off before the church hall, which they use as the church itself since they boarded the real church shut, although even that is unshuttered again, simply no longer a church. Nothing stays fixed here, which bothers Cairo. The boy runs along the path through the bungalows and out of sight.

Cairo turns left, along Watson's Green Road, into the gloom. He has the idea of running the opposite way up the hill, should meet the boy somewhere on Cawney Bank, the other side of the watershed, where the water slips down the hill and on and on to the River Severn and then out to sea and then back again as rain on the hills. At least he's got that knowledge and bets the kid does not.

Cairo never sees the boy from the front on these runs, only ever his heels, the bottoms of his shoes, his red back. He saw him in profile one morning when he had ducked down one of the entries on Lupin Road and disappeared. The way he holds his hands, poised. He must be in training, the way he runs on the balls of his feet, like it's nothing to get up these hills.

This is not even a boxing town. It is all football, of course, cricket in the old days. Cairo's great-grandad had helped build the County Ground in the thirties, but that is long gone too now. It is a fighting town, all right, that much is true. The hill is the thing that keeps you hanging on in the last seconds of a round, that keeps you upright.

At the turn he starts to breathe hard, not a great sign. He should've gone straight up the hill, cheating himself will bring no improvement. A patina of mud has come off the park and has slid across the pavement. Cairo takes care not to slip. He feels his feet against the ground as they push him upwards, feels a stone through his pump's thin sole, knows he could do with more protection, some decent running shoes. He has always felt heavier than he looks. It has helped him, his thick legs used to anchor him, let him soak up punishment. A dubious talent, for sure.

The breathing becomes easier again, going up towards the jagged outline of the new flats. He always thinks of them as that even though they are almost as old as he is, thirty-eight going on forty-five, split the difference.

Things are working out, Stacey-Ann in the house, his mom and dad's health steady, the babby with them. That there is a baby to replace another baby. That isn't how things work – after all, Zach is not his son but his grandson, he should not think this. But he knows deep down that he does.

The boy in the red hoodie has now gone. No sign of him. A ghost through the morning rain.

Cairo feels a sense of betrayal at this and he winds down the run as if he's a slowing clock.

Before

He ran further those mornings in the spring, through pains in his heel, his knees, the road unspooling beneath him. They had work, money coming in, he was paying Natalie off what he owed her, finally, had started to feel better about having had to borrow money from his ex-wife. He was getting up over the hill. He had started thinking about fighting again.

It's why he phoned Grace, he supposed, how he had the confidence to do it, confidence that had been gone for a long time. There had been something, when they spoke at the bottom of the marketplace, he wanted to say something, about the sense of his world being made invisible, mute, and he wanted to go against that. You had to fight your corner. That was something Alan and the others did not understand, even Tony. They ignored the world as it was and then felt angry with it. Not that he wasn't angry.

It was chance they finished up that day when they did, digging up the ground of the old abattoir, a big job that had paid something for once. Tony even seemed happy handing the money over.

One morning near the end of the job they dug up bones, wondered what to do with them, found a few scattered about the place, half a ribcage, a shallow, scattered grave. At first they thought the bones were human. What a fuss that would have created. They debated reburying them and saying nothing, until Alan pieced the skeleton together, the body of a pig, remnants of what used to go on there. Both Alan and Luke used to work there, when it was the abattoir, with the meat-packing factory next door. It had closed down years ago. Maybe the skeleton was of one last escapee. They used to make a run for it, Luke explained, the pigs were not stupid, knew what was coming to them, packed together in their dark lorries, herded down ramps into sterile factory buildings.

'I stood at my pork chop machine just about here,' Luke said, standing on the rutted ground. They had a break, sat on steel coils in a coven around the skeleton, toasted the pig with tea and bacon rolls that they sent one of the younger lads to fetch and laughed about, put the bones back in a trench they'd dug and covered them over. Everyone was happy because there was work and they were getting paid.

And that had been the feeling when he bumped into Grace, a roll of money in his pocket, and a gang of mates to have a drink with, and a roof over his head that wasn't going to disappear. That was how he felt that morning, so he could think about other things, was happy with what he'd said to her, 'Look around, people have had enough,' but not angry, apart from when she said it was all racism or because people were stupid. He could back up his theories, from afternoons spent with his old man at the local history groups, he was interested in all that stuff. Where we came from, where we were going. You had time to think, digging trenches, running up hills, and that was the hazard sometimes, you could think too much, so this was better, talking to a good-looking woman in the sunshine, spring here already, summer on its way, not so many summers left even if he lived into old age. Make the most of what you've got is what he told himself.

It went to voicemail when he phoned and he almost rang off. He was standing out the back, looking at the washing line, thinking he'd cut the grass for his dad, who insisted on hacking at it with an old pair of shears, the sagging fence and garage roofs, dandelions on the lawn, moss on the fence, the place seeping back into the hill.

'Hello, er, Grace. This is Cairo Jukes. We met in Dudley the other day. I wondered if. I'm interested in what you're filming. I think I could maybe say summat more, help you out maybe, I don't know. Give me a call if you think you might, you know. Well, thanks anyway.'

He regretted it straight away, ringing a girl like some kid asking to go out. It had been years since he had made a phone call where the person on the other end did not know what he was going to say. *I'm interested in what you're filming*, Jesus, like he knew anything about anything at all. He was a grandad.

His face was hot and he went inside and splashed water on it and tried to put the call out of his mind, but she phoned back and said she would love to meet up, that was what she said, and that she was back in Dudley, was staying at the new hotel by the cinema, and he said he could meet her there, said he would change from his work clothes as a joke that she didn't quite get, said that he lived not far away, which was true of course, although it all depended on how you measured these things.

After

Like the taste of coal in his mouth, a lump of coal, and the feeling of rain on his body. He is naked, here in the dark, in the cool rain, wishes he had never cursed it. He wishes it would rain now for ever.

They need the rain to stop to get paid for a full day. The job involves digging up pipes in Great Bridge, not far from where they dug up that pig. Everything above ground has gone, even the concrete floor of what had once been a factory building has disintegrated, so there is access to the pipes below the surface, copper and lead. They've dug a trench which has filled with water the length of the old factory wall, dug inwards to the pipes to wrench them out. The pipes worry him. There was that other place not far from here, somewhere in Tipton, where he pulled a length of copper off the wall and water had burst from it and then there he was with his finger stuck in the hole like in the story of the little Dutch boy at the dyke. He was left with one foot on the cherry picker and the other in mid-air.

Alan went on the phone to the Water Board fifty feet below him.

'Is it an emergency?' he'd heard Alan say, with a bit less urgency than he'd hoped for. Women worked on sewing machines down below him. They should not have been there at all. The gaffer, a white bloke, spoke to the women in their own language. The women giggled and opened umbrellas at their benches while it rained inside the ruined factory and Cairo clung to the pipe. He stayed there, had no choice, with the water coming through his clothes like he was some great cloud blown in from the Welsh hills and watched the level-crossing gates dip and rise for the trains from out of the dirty window. There was a blue sky beyond the streaks of bird shit. His arm went numb while he waited for them to find a stopcock. All he ended up with was a bollocking from Tony. The bloke had some nerve.

Alan whistles 'Singin' in the Rain' through his moustache as they hack away at the ground beneath their feet.

The Romanians are already at work. They strike an expanse of concrete with picks. Cairo does not know to what end, for pipes buried there too, or Saxon gold. He sees their heads lift to watch the rich man's car pass. Tony comes by most mornings to check up on them. The Romanians stand in their hats and hoods in the rain. One of the older men wipes his hands on a rag, looks at the gaffer's car. They are not even Romanian. They are from Moldova, the man drying his hands speaks some English, told Cairo when they stood around waiting for the vans to turn up late one darkening Friday afternoon early in the year. 'Moldova,' he'd said, like some country from a storybook. It is the same with the Albanians. Cairo has not seen them for a while. They come from Kosovo, call themselves Albanian, these men who worked in the sleet last winter, have been through wars, who disappear in the mist.

Tony does not even turn off the engine. He sits for a while and watches them get wet, then opens the window to call Alan over. Cairo watches Alan's face in Tony's mirrored glasses. Why does he need sunglasses when it's pissing down with rain? And he can see, as Alan's eyes narrow and his face creases and droops with his moustache, that Tony is telling them to knock off, even though everyone knows that the rain will blow over. Tony wants to save a day's money and Cairo can feel a sickness rising in him. He'll be a day short now this week. He worries about Nat, what he might say to her, the money, she works out interest on what he owes her. He could stay out of the way, he supposes, the broken phone makes that easier.

Men like Tony are never skint. These men have cash-flow problems, issues with liquidity and leverage and solvency, words Cairo knows but has no clue as to their meaning, doesn't want to either. You can cover anything with words. They are never plain-out skint, but he bets that Tony hasn't got the money to pay them the full week, is using the rain as his excuse.

He watches Alan nod his head again, sign for their money a day short, plus a tenner for getting soaked this morning, not even with a pen. Alan traces his name onto the screen of Tony's phone, some gimmick Tony has started using, even though he pays them all in dog-eared notes in cash bags from the post office like they are men from some bygone era. Like they are men who would go walking up the lane here from this factory back when it was still standing, men with an early Friday finish, going to tend their allotments and stand up at bars and walk their dogs and go home to their families and fill in the football coupon and dream of a week at the seaside. As if there is any of that any more.

Cairo spits into the trench at his feet, looks up again with the rest of the men as they watch Tony drive away across the wasteland. The car has the same shine as his glasses, reflects the pockmarked ground and shapes of the men standing there in the dying rain. The hole in Cairo's right boot has filled with water. He hopes Tony hits a puddle, splashes mud up the bodywork, but he'd only get it cleaned, leave it sitting there shining on the drive of his house up in Oakham, like no one knows where he comes from, like he isn't who he is, has become something else.

He'd lamped Tony once, when they were kids, Cairo had. Given him a right paling, as they used to say. There'd been some feud about something, he can't remember what, and Cairo had thumped him, blacked his eye, wished he'd thrown him in the cut now, held his head under the water. He remembers one of their lads saying, 'Yome in trouble now, Cairo, that's one of the Clanceys,' and him saying that he did not give a shit, even though he was scared to go anywhere for a month afterwards, until some sort of truce was brokered. They were mates then for a while. Tony even got them that modelling work. They had to pose on the towpath down at Windmill End, by the tunnel mouth and Cobb's Engine House, wearing clothes from the Littlewoods catalogue. He wonders if Tony can even remember that, half a life and more away now. Money lets you forget everything. Tony Clancey in his German car and his *Leave* sticker, in his Italian shirts, with his English attitudes, with Cairo's ex-wife and sometimes his daughter and sometimes his grandson, a man who has taken his family, no better than any one of the men standing here in the rain, no better, drives off to his golf club to wait for the rain to stop.

Before

'So like a documentary?'

They sat in the hotel bar at Castle Gate. She had gone back to London, come back again for another visit. He stood in front of the narrow wardrobe mirror, tried on a couple of different shirts. The name of the place was new, the whole development, cinema and gym and diner and so on, like it was bloody California. Well, twenty years or so new. They were on the edge of where the old County Ground had been, which Cairo's grandad helped to build, had worked on the building of the zoo as well, had been a quarryman there in the castle pits. His dad told him he used to get sent to fetch the old man back when he was a kid, would find him in a deckchair by the side of the old pavilion, tucked away out of the wind watching Tom Graveney, George Headley, sipping his mild ale. Cairo used to sneak onto the site as a kid with his mates, after it had been abandoned, unsafe with the collapses. They would run through the long grass, bounce on the twisted metal fences that were put up to keep the kids and the tatters out, but had fallen or been pulled down. There were pictures of dogs but no dogs. Perhaps they'd fallen in the holes. Cairo would imagine the ground shifting beneath his feet, the world swallowing them all up.

'Yes, trying to show how people feel like they have lost out.'

She looked at him across the table. He seemed younger, out of his work clothes, his hair parted and free from dust. They were closer in age than she had first assumed, although it was hard to tell. He was talking about the 1830s, cholera, the digging of trenches and pits, the digging of tunnels, like he had actually been there. She could ask him, of course. There was a loose thread that came from the top button of his shirt and she wanted to reach out to it.

'I doh think they feel like they've lost out. They have lost out.'

'Isn't that the same thing?'

'No, thass part of the problem, thinking that it is. We'm sitting on one of the places we've lost. You make out like it's our problem, it's only about how we feel, but we have lost, it doh really matter what we feel about it. It's a fact. You can prove it.'

'What can you prove?'

'The loss, actual loss. Jobs, houses, security, all them things.' He paused. 'But maybe yome right that there's the feelings as well, of loss, of having lost.'

He had never spoken about things in quite this way, would ramble on sometimes when he'd had a drink, but who was there to even listen to him these days? He knew the history. He was named for an ancestor who had dug the Netherton Tunnel, fought bare knuckle. His old man had folders full of family stories, local history, used to lead walks along the cut, through the tunnels, would tell stories as he went, would send articles with hand-drawn maps and sketches to the *Bugle*, the *Blackcountryman*. Sometimes Cairo's mother used to tell him to stop harking back. 'Yow have to know where yow've come from to know where yome headed,' is what his dad said. Cairo considered that it might be better not to know at all where they were headed, given where it seemed to be.

The idea of loss conjured up his boxing, and that is what he had been, a boxer with a losing record, some-one people would book for fights because he made other fighters look good, would last, make them work, give people what they wanted, which was not the same as being no good at it, not at all. He waited for the chance to say to Grace, 'When I was a boxer...'

'I think you're right, Cairo, that there is a culture here that has been neglected, forgotten,' which is what she had come to believe, and was why she was here, she told herself. Her own family had come through this way, after all, which is why she picked the town in the first place. Near the end, her dad had become obsessed with trac-ing his family's roots. He had spent his academic career writing about Roman slaves, the empire's industries, about the invisible men ('And women too,' she heard her mother's voice say) who mined the lead, who hammered the chains, where they came from, who they were. It was only at the very end, when he came home from hospital to lie in bed and look out of the window at the trees on the Heath, that she understood that this work had also been about himself. He traced the routes his ancestors took, from pirate ships and Cornish coves and tin mines, to Devon as weavers, north to Kidderminster for more work, into the Black Country as iron masters, then south to Oxford and London. On family holidays they had walked by glittering waters, on Tresco, on Bryher, imagined the tide sweeping them away, the edges of the islands, the Continent.

'Like on the telly and that, the papers, just being told we'm all stupid, held up for ridicule.'

'What?'

'Like with the wheel.'

He tapped the front of the newspaper. Grace was the one who'd bought the paper with the headline about the town's new Ferris wheel.

'These people have got it coming,' he said with a feeling she found hard to understand. This man she had known for a few hours, less. She surprised herself when she noticed no wedding ring, not that it meant anything. They had talked so far of fathers and newspaper stories.

'Which people?'

'The people who write this crap.'

'But they want people to vote leave, most of the papers do.'

'Iss just a game to them, a funny game, like life's a game. I bet the people writing these papers don't vote to leave, I bet they live in fancy houses in London and they'll vote to stay. They'm all doing fine, thank you very much. It's like a double bluff.'

'Who's playing games now?'

'You get what I mean, though?'

'I'm not sure I do. You mean that people here will vote against whatever they think the perceived elite will vote?'

'Here you go again. It ay perceived. There is an elite.'

'But some of the elite want you to vote to leave.'

'They doh mean it.'

'What do you mean, they don't mean it?'

'I've told yer, it's all a game of double bluff. They'll all argue about it. We'll have the vote. It'll be a vote to stay in. They'll fix it if they need to. Then they'll get on with whatever's next on the agenda, all mates together again.'

'I think they mean it, and anyway, what, it's all one big conspiracy?'

'You said it. A conspiracy of the elite, thass your word by the way, these are your own words, against the rest of us. You should write this down, put it in your film.'

'I will.' She suddenly had to laugh.

'You should be paying me for this stuff, it's gold dust.' His face broke out into a broad smile. 'You'll probably win another prize.' His indignation seemed to have blown itself out.

She had made sure she told him about the Balkan film, the prize they had won for it. She wanted to signal to him that she was a professional film-maker, their relationship was a professional one. She did not want to think of him as an attractive man. After all, he might be picking up on it, getting the wrong idea.

He paused for a moment, then added, 'You got time for another drink?'

'I have, why not? Thank you.'

He came back with two bottles of beer.

'Cheers.' He tilted his bottle towards her. 'What I'm saying is that this place used to be somewhere.' He took a sip of his beer. 'And still could be,' he added, but sounded less sure about that.

After

The door knocker rattles through the house. Stacey-Ann would never go to the door when in on her own, but she does wonder for a moment if it is Duane. This thought is a surprise to her. Zach kicks his legs on the changing mat and she gets up from her knees and crouches at the upstairs window, peers above the ledge through the net, smiles at her own ridiculousness. She cannot see the door but the knocker goes again with some urgency. A dog barks nearby at the noise. She has heard of a scam lately, someone at the front door saying they are from the council, and then someone round the back breaking in. For what? A bit of change, most likely. Money for kids' sweets or the bingo. She would not go to the door, but it worries her that her nan might, if in on her own, no matter how many times you tell her not to. Her nan and grandad are up the road collecting a prescription. Stacey-Ann asked her nan to stay in. But she got her walker and said she wanted to talk to the pharmacist. Out of pure stubbornness.

'Stacey-Ann.' It is her mother's voice. Is she in the house? Maybe she has a key, after all these years, an old key she has kept. Stacey-Ann waits to hear her on the stairs.

'Stacey-Ann, I know yome in there, love. I want to speak to yer. This is ridiculous.'

The letter box, of course. She is talking through the letter box. Stacey-Ann pictures her mom crouched down there on the path and this pleases her for a moment, more than it should. Zach begins to make loud squeaking noises, kicks his legs on the changing mat, and Stacey-Ann crawls across the bedroom and giggles and shushes the boy. Alert now, she hears her mother on the path below, footsteps, high-heeled boots. When she creeps back to the window she sees her mother standing there by the gate, looking up at the house. Her mother narrows her eyes. She needs glasses and doesn't wear them. Stacey-Ann feels confident she will not notice her here, hidden under the window, but half wants her to. She must have watched the house, to know she is in on her own with Zach. He shouts out again, a laugh. He is a happy baby. This must have taken a lot, for her mom to have done this. Her mom is not a woman to change her mind, to admit she might have been wrong. And Stacey-Ann decides to go down and let her mom in. But before she has time to turn from the window, she watches as her mother's shoulders slump and the woman turns and goes through the gate, leaving it open, which will annoy Grandad, and then disappears on the other side of the hedge, the clack of her heels receding. And after a moment there is the sound of a car starting.

Stacey-Ann picks up Zach and carries him downstairs carefully, half expects her mother's face to loom up at the window. Her grandparents have left the telly on with the sound off, a habit they have got into, so that if anyone does look through the window it might convince them there are people in the house. A quiz show plays. Subtitles appear on the screen. Her nan watches the telly with subtitles now. But when her dad's interview came on telly, they played subtitles for everyone to read, like he wasn't speaking English at all, and she saw it grieved him when he watched it, but he just shrugged his shoulders when she asked him about it. 'What do you expect?' he said.

Grace said that she would be back over the summer and Stacey-Ann took her at her word, and then emailed and texted, but she has had no reply. The summer has faded. Grace said she would find out about college stuff for her, or find someone who could. It isn't as if Stacey-Ann is desperate and, anyway, she could find all this stuff for herself, she isn't stupid, but it's more like the thing itself is important, the contact. Grace had been someone nice to talk to, someone different, even though Stacey-Ann only stayed that time because all the other mothers left, had places to go to, or said they did, put their heads down and didn't look at the pretty woman with the posh accent, as if they were ashamed of something. It's not that not getting back to her would let her,

Stacey-Ann, down. No. Stacey-Ann doesn't want Grace to let herself down.

When her dad was on the teatime news, Stacey-Ann said as little as possible. They showed him talking to Grace by Dudley marketplace. 'People have had enough,' is what he said, with or without subtitles, talking about the EU, like he knew much about it. For all she knows, he does. He knows a lot about history, her grandad too, but more like little stories, like the Tipton Slasher and his pet monkey. Her dad used to make up stories about the monkey to get her to sleep when she was a kid. The monkey was called Ronaldo, he said, like the footballer. She wants to ask him to tell those stories to Zach as he grows. They will be all right, of that she will make sure, and she thinks if she mentions the stories to her dad he'll see that they'll be all right. Although he's got his own worries.

And she doesn't agree with him, her dad, not about the vote anyway. Not that she's about to launch into any big debate with him about it, they've got other more important things to think about, but it's not right, all this carrying on about foreigners, people moving on to get a better life, although she doesn't understand herself, not really, it's not like you can believe politicians, they are just in it for themselves. Maybe the foreign politicians are as bad as our own. They might be worse. You couldn't think people were better because they were foreign. Some people did, teachers they'd had at school. There's just another kind of prejudice.

Stacey-Ann wishes it had been Duane at the door, and again the wish surprises her. She thinks she hears her mother's heels on the path again and stands at the window and there is no one there. A lone bee veers above the front garden. She can hear the traffic, distant on the main road.

She doesn't agree with her dad, or her other dad, Tony, in fact, who's worse than her real dad about this kind of thing. He really is racist. Just wrong. She wonders how he thinks he can say the things he does when there's a brown baby there in front of him, or not in front of him during these last few months, that he wants to call him Grandad, even though he is really nothing of the sort. They've got a *Leave* poster up in the front garden on one of those boards that the estate agents use. She asked her mom what she thought and she said she didn't know anything about it. Her dad, her real dad, thinks her mom is only interested in things, in the house and the cars and what she looks like. He might be right. Still, it's good to have a nice house, to not have to worry about things so much, so that's not such a terrible crime either. Her mother is jealous of baby Zach, that's what it comes down to. That's why she threw her, Stacey-Ann, out of the house and told her to go back to her dad, her real dad.

The sound of boots on the path, she is certain this time. Even the sound of the boots are important to her mom, they have to sound expensive, say something about her place in the world, where she is going, the distance she has come. The letter box rattles and Stacey-Ann stands dead still, can't decide whether to move or not, and hears the boots on the path again. The boots sound impatient. She pulls back the curtain this time, watches her mom as she walks away.

The college idea is all to do with moving on. Stacey-Ann has this fantasy that she wants to collect exams like her mom collects boots. She had thought she was stuck, having packed in sixth form, gone to work at the salon. Grace had said there were access courses, that you didn't have to do A-levels or go to college full-time to go to university. And Stacey-Ann felt stupid for not really having grasped this before. Although she did know it, she knew people found ways of making things happen. Other people.

'I think people could be a bit kinder to each other, a bit less judgemental,' is what she'd said to Grace when she came to the new mothers' group. She wasn't filming then. She'd said that she was here to ask some questions if anyone was willing to stay, and that was when the others all rushed off, put their heads down and looked at the floor, so Stacey-Ann stayed to talk to her out of a sense of kindness. There was a feeling that the people who mattered, the ones Grace really wanted to talk to, had left.

She told her her name was Ann, realized too late it was because she wanted to impress this woman, was ashamed of the way Stacey-Ann might sound to a woman like Grace. Realized the irony that she was sitting in the clinic, nineteen years old, with a baby on her lap, thrown out of her mother's house and no sign of the dad, so if anyone wanted to make judgements it wasn't her name she need worry about. And Grace gave her a card with her name on it and email and number, like that was the most natural thing in the world.

So Stacey-Ann gave her one in return, one from the salon that she dug from her purse, *Puerto Rico Nail and Tan Bar*, *Rowley Village*, and she scribbled her number and email address on it like she sometimes does for customers. Did. She is not working. She says she is on maternity leave, but it all comes down to whether her mother will have her back in the house, let alone the shop. Whether she will go back if she asks her. Which is what she imagines this rattling on the door is all about.

Zach is on his play mat. In a while she will put him in his pram, go for a walk along the quiet roads, towards the park, so he can look at the tree branches above him. There's an envelope on the doormat, she picks it up, her name, her mother's writing. Thinks she'll put the kettle on first, put Zach in his rocker.

When she emailed Grace she had considered writing, *You interviewed my dad and it was on the telly*, but thought better of it. And when her dad said he'd been interviewed she didn't tell him that she had too because he seemed so pleased about it, like literally more happy about it than anything for years, apart from Zach. He was happy about being a grandad and she was proud of that. Proud of her own dad, if that was possible, like she was the parent. Except not of what he said about the voting. He was too negative. It was because of his own experiences, of course, but he shouldn't apply his own life like it was a rule. He'd been unlucky. It made her feel disloyal thinking about him like this, but it was the truth. Tony said you made your own luck in the world. She didn't agree. Her mother was wrong to think that Zach was a mistake of some kind. Even though she didn't see Duane, that was true. Things might come good there. And if not, she would look after Zach, and who knows for the future? You couldn't tell.

She looks at the envelope. She picks up Zach, holds him on her hip and opens the front door, walks down the path with him and shuts the gate. She picks up the envelope on the way back in.

Before

He tried to see the house through her eyes, understood that he could not. There was blossom in the air and a breeze that came through the screen of trees at the back of the houses, cottages you might even call them, that sounded like the sea. The hydrangeas had started to flower early. The new people at the end of the row had left a settee half on the pavement for collection.

He looked at Grace, looked away, ushered her up the path, berated himself again about whatever it was that had taken hold of him. She said she was looking for people to interview, for background, a portrait of the place, not opinions, more like stories, layers, depths, the way things had been, the ways they had changed. He said his parents would be perfect. The word parents was strange in his mouth, he was not sure he had ever used it, only ever said 'Mom and Dad', and he only really meant his dad. 'Yow must be joking, Cairo,' is what his mother said. He had not used the front door since the day of his nan's funeral, years ago, he always

53

went up the entry, round the back. His dad opened the door before they got to it. His mother stood behind in the hall, shadowy, holding a plate of biscuits.

Grace held her hand out for his dad to shake and he worried for a moment that the man would not take it, would not know what to do, but of course he took her hand and asked her in.

'I love your hydrangeas,' Grace said.

His dad smiled, things would be all right. She was a woman who said she loved things very easily. The hydrangeas were all right, could have done with tidying up a bit. His old man had not stopped moaning about them all week.

They sat in the front room. Grace and Cairo sat. His mother hovered at the doorway. His dad stood with his back to the wall while they drank their tea and took biscuits from the plate that sat on the heavily polished table under the window. The light filtered through the net curtains.

Cairo stood up to get his dad to sit down, all so awkward, squeezed himself against his dad's belly as he came to the chair. They could have done this in the back, had more space, but of course they had to use the best room. Grace set the camera up. His dad sat down heavily in the armchair. Cairo trod carefully into the hall and pulled the door behind him.

'What a lovely-looking girl,' his mom said.

He could hear Grace saying something to his dad. Then his dad talked to the camera, in a voice he did not fully recognize.

'I worked at the same foundry for thirty-one years, from aged fifteen to when I was forty-six,' he heard him say, then crept backwards down the hall to the kitchen, looking at the lines of the wallpaper as he went, noticed the way there was a light socket they'd never trimmed the paper from properly, told himself he might finish it that afternoon.

He wiped the cups that his mother had already washed. She sat now to drink her own cup of tea, dip a biscuit. A blackbird flitted around outside the window. He stood at the doorway to listen, could hear his dad talking, in full flow now.

'You'd look out at night and all you could see was light – fires from the furnaces, you know, as far as you could see, the place all lit up. There was work for all the men. Man's work, not like now. I know that's something yow ay meant to say any more, so forgive me. There was a culture that went alongside the work. And doh get me wrong, for the most part it had been a hard life. I'm the youngest of ten. Me brothers and sisters was born all through the twenties and thirties and they used to talk about how things was. I had other brothers and sisters who died as babbies. After the war it was easier, for a bit, for a long time, I suppose, when they built these houses, others like em, and we all moved up from the town. My ancestors was nailers and puddlers and coal-pickers and navvies and so on. They dug canals and tunnels. My ode mon dug rock out the hill under the castle. None of them jobs exist no more. They ay done for years. Maybe that's a good thing. Folks had hard lives. And things am easier now. Some things am easier. Although you wouldn't think it, some of the things that have happened, some of the stuff the young uns face now. What I'm saying is you shouldn't wish it back, but we never wished for the way things am today either. We need to start afresh, change direction.'

'What's he saying now?' his mother asked from the kitchen table.

'The way things was, Mom, all the works and that, you know.'

'The usual,' she said. 'I doh see the point of keep looking back, Cairo, I really doh. I've told him, get on with things. Stop pestering about things that have gone. Concentrate on what's here.' She looked out of the window at the listing back fence.

'I know, Mom, I know,' he said.

While the man talked Grace looked at the framed photographs on the wall. She had been looking at the girl for a while before she recognized her. It was the girl she had spoken to at the doctor's surgery, what was her name? There were photos of the baby, too, in white knitted clothes, and even as she looked at them, she could not make the link between Cairo and the girl with the baby, which reminded her she said she would speak to her again, while the man talked about fires as far as the eye could see.

When they finished, and she'd thanked him and was packing away the camera, she motioned to the photos on the wall. 'That's a beautiful baby,' she said.

'Me great-grandson,' the man said. 'They'll be back in a bit. Zachariah, the babby's named. Thass Stacey-Ann, me granddaughter, Cairo's daughter.' He pushed himself up from the chair.

'You have a lovely family, Mr Jukes,' she said.

He looked at her for a moment as if trying to work out the joke.

After

They trudge up the slope towards the access road.

'I swear to God this rain's already easing off,' Luke says.

He and Cairo hold opposite ends of a tarpaulin, kindling and rags and a can of petrol sloshing about in the hammock that they have formed. Alan walks next to them, hands in his pocket. They were meant to have burnt the rubbish this afternoon, anything they couldn't use, but it was too damp to do it now and would have to wait. Cairo is not sure such fires are allowed any more, whether they ever were, and is dubious about why they might be burning things on Tony's behalf, destroying evidence of some kind. Luke says he'll take the stuff and keep it in his car, keep it dry.

'What did he say to yer?' Cairo asks Alan.

'Just said it was setting in, the rain, that we was best to finish now. The drainage on there's fucked anyway. We'll be knee deep in water.'

'What's he, a weatherman now as well as everything else? Some kind of fucking drainage engineer.'

Alan does not say anything. Instead he passes Cairo his pay packet. Cairo grips the tarpaulin in the other hand. He holds the money tight in his fist. The veins bulge and he pictures his fists wrapped, gloved, the minutes before a fight starts, before that first bell sounds.

'Says we might be finishing up here next week any road.' Drops of water are trapped in Alan's moustache.

'Did he say anything about more work?'

Alan says nothing.

'Fucking hell,' Cairo says, and he hears the panic in his own voice, and he wishes he'd shut up, wishes he did not always give himself away. He'd be no poker player, that much is certain. That is one avenue closed to him.

'Coming up Dudley after?' Alan says.

'I thought yow was banned?'

Alan shrugs. 'Come up this after, if yer fancy.'

'I might,' Cairo says.

There are snails on the path in the rain. Cairo steps carefully to miss them, as they carry the tarpaulin to Luke's car. He can feel his ankle, there might be something wrong with the pins that hold his joint in place, like they are coming loose or rusting or something. He limps at the end of most days, tries to run with it strapped up, knows that this cannot be doing it much good. He sees a snail smashed under a boot up in front of them, walks past another which is still moving, struggling, dying, with half of itself squashed and oozing in a trail behind it, the shell smashed to bits. He cannot bring himself to step on it and put the thing out of its misery. He is sure the new kid ahead of them is stamping on the snails on purpose.

'Watch them snails,' he shouts out to the kid.

'What?'

'I said watch them snails. Step round em.'

The boy stops, turns, looks at him, waits for Cairo to laugh, but he doesn't.

'Am yer joking?'

'No, I ay fucking joking. Watch where yome walking.'

'Yow watch who yome talking to.'

'All right, Cairo, eh? Don't worry, mate. Don't worry, our kid.' Alan has his arm around Cairo. The boy weighs things up for a moment before turning and carrying on up the track.

'Fucking hell, Cairo. Calm down, eh?'

'Why would yer stamp on the fucking snails though? They'm living things, fuck's sake.'

Luke veers with the tarpaulin and keeps Cairo's hands busy, and the boy carries on up the road in front of them. Cairo sees the shape of his back, the way he holds himself. Looks like the boy from Lupin Road.

'Let me know if yer need the motor later, Cairo. I'm gonna drop it back and then go for a drink,' Luke says, and Cairo knows Luke is trying to keep him talking, sees the kid glaring at him from the top of the slope.

'Ta, mate, I'm probably stopping in,' he says, ignores the boy.

This arrangement has lasted years now. Cairo is not supposed to drive, had his licence revoked when he had that fit after the series of concussions, after his last fights, ten years or so now. Has felt fine with all that for years, more or less, but has never tried to get the licence back. He uses Luke's car when he needs to, walks over the hill to pick it up from where Luke parks it outside his back gate, fills it up with petrol or slips him a twenty every now and again, when they get paid for a full week. He has even taken his mother to a hospital appointment in it a few times. Everyone turns a blind eye. It helps Luke out a bit, he's got his own troubles, although the car will not last much longer, a battered red Peugeot 206 with a big dent in the back passenger door. He breathes in the smell of the petrol as they fold the tarpaulin into the car boot.

'Want a lift?' Luke asks.

'No, mate. I'm gooin the other way,' he says, although he isn't.

He shouts ta-ra to the others. The kid has stopped looking.

'Duane, come,' says one of the other young lads. The name registers dully with Cairo. He is not sure why.

Alan calls Cairo back and presses a fiver into his hand and tells him to get summat for the babby, must know he's short.

Cairo turns left without really thinking, the wrong direction to get home, but at least out of the way of the pub, and talk of the pub, towards Great Bridge, with the traffic idling at the lights, some people still on their way to work, and he, Cairo, already finished up for the day.

And it almost feels good, to have no work to go to, to feel the day open up in front of him. The rain has eased, there is a lighter grey to the sky over Dudley Castle, even some shreds of blue from where the weather comes. Cairo can do without the pub, that wait for them to open up, then sitting there all day and watching the light change through the bar as time passes, a game of pool, something to eat, pissing your money away. Alan does not care. He sits out on the benches with a few cans when the pubs refuse to serve him, does not care who comes past, gets his shirt off if the sun breaks through, shouts hello if he sees anyone looking over at him. Cheerful, everyone's mate, until at some point that switches and he is everyone's enemy, including his own. Get down the road before that happens, that is Cairo's advice to the kids hanging round him, even Duane, this kid from Lupin Road who can skip up the hill away from him and will not look away from his stare. Not that anyone asks his advice.

And not that he is not Alan's mate. The other week he'd gone out with him, down West Brom, because Alan had gone to see his ex-missus first, and they had started in the Wetherspoon's, there in the old snooker hall, and gradually worked their way back up the hill. Some mad fucker had stood on a table of a pub he couldn't remember the name of, backstreets, off Carters Green, and had sung Wolves songs at the top of his voice and everyone threw stuff at him. Cairo and Alan had come laughing up the road, rolling drunk and shocked to find it was only teatime. Later, they sat in Alan's front room, what had been his front room, all the windows boarded up and two deckchairs facing where the telly used to be. Cairo started to tell Alan about Grace then, had to talk to someone about it or he'd go crazy, looked across at Alan asleep in his deckchair with his shirt off, a smoking ashtray on one side of him, a tumbler with his glass eye sitting in it on the other, and he sneaked out, threw up into the hedge, swore never again.

That is Alan's party trick, taking his eye out. He'd lost it, had it glassed out in a big fight with the Gypsies back when they were kids. And the thing is Alan does not care, does not give a shit, as he happily tells anyone who might ask, a bit too forcefully if you want Cairo's opinion. His missus and his kids have gone, his furniture too, eviction notices and court summonses make a carpet across the hall, that moustache just grows longer and scraggier, and if you ask him how he is he says all right, mate, or shrugs his shoulders, or tells you he couldn't give a shit.

'What yer talking to her for?' Alan had asked him, when he did the interview in the marketplace. The interview and everything else. He pictured her in the room for a moment, standing by the mirrored wardrobes, tries to push that image away. He had wanted to say to Alan it was so that he could speak to the woman with the long hair and the microphone and the soft skin, because when would someone like that ever speak to someone like them, smile at blokes like them? Grace, her name was Grace, but Alan knew that well enough and had already called her a stuck-up bitch and walked off up the High Street.

'About the vote, y'know, the Europe vote.'

'I doh know nothing about that,' Alan said.

'Have yer ever voted?' Cairo asks him.

'Have I fuck.'

See, could not give a shit. Whereas Cairo had always been proud to vote, had it drummed into him by his old man.

'And a fat lot of use it's always done yer,' is what Alan said to him. 'Have a look around yer, sunshine. See what good voting does.'

It had been Cairo she wanted to speak to anyway, Grace, not to Alan, not to Luke or the others. When did any of them ever speak to women called Grace? Although not even that is true, because he remembers his mom has a cousin called Gracie, who owned an Alsatian and had a caravan at Bromyard. Still, Gracie, not Grace. He knows that makes the difference.

Before

The wheel went faster than Grace imagined it would, like an old-fashioned fairground ride. There were kids running around at the base of it, laughing and shrieking, Friday afternoon. The children held biscuits with smiley faces done in icing or chocolate, the brown and white faces of the biscuits chased the brown and white faces of the children, and they laughed and whirled in the square below. He told her that when they put the wheel up in Birmingham the commentary that played was in French, described what you might see as you rose above Paris. Said people wanted to keep it on, how you could hear about the Champs-Élysées as you looked across the Midlands traffic. There was no commentary here, the wind suddenly whipped against you when you were carried above the buildings.

Up and over the pub below, *The Saracen's Head and Freemasons' Arms*, said the austere lettering, and what history was locked in that name? she wondered. This had been his boxing club, he told her. Saracens, there by the potato merchants, steps that went down into the gloom of potato dust and the lights of the gym. He told her that the club had been forced to change its name from the Saracen's Head, move away from the badge of a bearded, decapitated man, in order to gain some funding. Political correctness, he said, in the same deadpan tone as he described taking Paris for Birmingham, as if he was mentioning a change in the weather, and he maintained his stare as he said it, and she hadn't said anything at all and nodded. He said he didn't go to the club any more anyway, but it meant something to him.

It was very green around the castle, which came into view like exposed bone, over the pub roof, and so were the hills that rippled away from the edge of the town. When she came back she would film at the zoo in the castle grounds. She wanted images of llamas, parrots, giraffes, and the soundtrack of people lamenting what they'd lost, the shrieks of children playing and laughing all at the same time. There was something definite now, some shape to what she was doing. There was a BBC producer she had to ring back about Cairo's interview, they might want to use it. The wind blew as they reached the top of the arc and she looked through the wheel's white mesh and leaned against him as they dipped back towards the buildings.

'This is all right,' is what he said, but with genuine inflection in his voice, a sense of delight in it. The children's cries came back, the sounds of happy people.

There were things here that did not add up, that's what she felt. She stayed leaned into him as they dipped and rose again.

He told her that this was a hill country of long views. He had taken her to the top of the hill, the bank as he had called it, looked out towards Malvern, said there had once been a viewing platform where they stood, a watchtower with a telescope at the top, built to look for the French when Napoleon threatened invasion. You could see the sea then, he said, Lundy Island out there in the choppy brown water between England and Wales. There had been carnivals on the bank and people queued to go up and have a look. Later there had been a plan to build the world's tallest building on the site of the old steelworks, where the shopping centre was.

'You're making this up,' she said.

'You couldn't make that up,' is what he said in return.

She thought back to the newspapers. Something did seem weirdly amiss, about a country that might ridicule such an innocent thing as a big wheel turning above the buildings of a town, to dismiss the view of the hills beyond, some deep fissure that was about more than fairground rides and innocent ways to pass ten minutes in the springtime blossom in England.

Afterwards they sat in the Saracen's Head at a table near the window. They could see the wheel as it turned, the children gone home now. People drifted across the square, workers from the council offices nearby. When the pub door opened he would glance up at it, watch whoever came in as they walked to the bar, then turn his attention back to Grace. He picked at the edge of a beer mat.

'You OK?' she said. And after a pause, 'Thank you for this afternoon. You've really helped me with all this. I appreciate it.'

She had assumed that to come to the pub was a good idea, but now she was not so sure, the way he looked through the window to the door, back again, picked at the beer mat. She had asked him about the gym, the club, whether they could call in there, and he'd said, 'Leave it with me,' but it was possible that was it. He said he'd been away from all that for a long time.

The last time he was in here was years ago. He and Nat used to come here, Saturday nights, and if he was in training he'd drink cordial and soda water and stand straight-backed near the doors and let people look over and nod towards him, and sometimes people would come up and shake his hand and ask him when he was next fighting and it had felt good, to be somebody. Now he could see his reflection in the window where they sat, Grace next to him, and he didn't want to see anyone who knew him. There's Cairo Jukes, that old boxer, people might say, if they said anything at all, making a fool of himself with that woman, look. Must think he's summat pretty special.

'Would you like another drink?' she asked, motioned to the pint he'd drunk and not tasted.

He'd got the car, which was another reason not to drink, and he had money in his pocket, but there was the money he owed Natalie and what he needed to give to Luke, should at least fill the car up with petrol, turn up a bit of rent at home, slip Stacey-Ann something for Zachariah. He should stay out of the pub. 'Women like that, they'm bad news, mate, in the end,' is what Luke had said. Luke wasn't a headcase, not like Alan. Even Luke, giving him a kind of warning.

'I'll get one,' he said, and stood up.

'No, let me,' she said, and it angered him suddenly, the ease of all this, the ease with which she sat here and then offered to buy him drinks and looked at him like she did, from her world that was not his. Easy come, easy go. She might go back to London tonight, she might not. All so simple. She put her hand on his, smiled at him, and he felt the anger shift in him again, the churn of it, the way it came and went and became other things. He wanted her to leave her hand on his. Looked at her, but she had already turned to go to the bar. He shifted in the chair, watched the sun on the square outside, tried to enjoy things while they were here.

She wanted to tell him she could put it on the film's budget, claim some sort of expenses, but there was no budget of course. She assumed it was that she got the drinks that annoyed him, although he seemed reassured now, sitting back at the table.

'There's a place,' she said when she sat back down, 'an Indian restaurant, I've got an address for it. It's quite near, I think. I know some of the UKIP activists meet there on a Friday night, someone I spoke to. I wondered if you fancied going. I mean, if you're not busy or anything later. I could call the people I spoke to, but I thought I might go and have a look around. Anyway, I haven't had a curry here, people have said to, what with the reputation for it and everything. It might be fun.'

What swayed him was when she said it might be fun. She actually used the word fun. She was a person who used words such as fun and wonderful, and he was not sure he'd ever met anyone who spoke like this in real life, or anywhere else for that matter. It seemed to open something up. Maybe it was OK, changing again after years, to feel himself becoming someone new, when he'd assumed he'd shrink away.

She mentioned the name Jamie Iqbal and it made him laugh. She said something earnest about how one strategy of the party, of the far right in general, in order to legitimize itself, was to use people of colour. That was the phrase she used, people of colour, and he remembered it as something strange. Zachariah was a person of colour, Cairo was not. Was that what it meant? Jamie Iqbal was indeed a person of colour. The idea that people like Grace thought certain politics were illegitimate, and how that might make those politics more appealing to other people, that was what she didn't get. People were sick of being told what to think and not think. He would try to explain that to her. Again. Not here though, not right now.

'I know Jamie, was mates with him once, I suppose. It'll be him using them, doh worry about that.'

For a moment he had been concerned that it might have been Tony she'd been talking to, it was possible, but there was part of him that would not have worried at all about bumping into Tony and Natalie, UKIP activists if that was what they were now, if that was what you called them, with Grace standing next to him, the way he might look them in the eye and they could pay him a bit of the respect he was due, their jaws would probably drop open. Instead of laughing at him. He knew they did, that he was yesterday's man and they ridiculed him, if they talked about him at all.

He saw himself again reflected in the window. Imagined the man there getting up, taking Grace's hand, walking off into a different life altogether.

The restaurant was on a back road in the Lye, on an industrial estate, not too promising. Cairo could see the railway viaduct that came out of Stourbridge over the grey warehouses, the sky already underlit with orange street lights. It was later than he would have liked.

In the paper Jamie talked about running gala nights, big crowds, at this new place. People could eat their curry ringside and watch the fights, and there would be singers, cabaret between the bouts. Jamie, shameless, said he planned to bring a bit of Las Vegas to the Black

Country, which made Cairo laugh when his dad passed him the *Dudley News*, and said, 'Have yer seen what your mate's doing now?' But, still, it was something to think about. Though he wondered about Grace, asking questions.

'Like they don't have cab firms here,' she said to him, smiling when he'd insisted on driving, a couple of pints in, and he should be careful, he understood that.

'It ay like London, you know,' he said, wasn't really sure what he meant by this and was glad she didn't press him on it. When he'd had those fights in London, the people had been much the same as at home. This woman was none of those things, in her patterned dress and cardigan and masses of hair and ideas that things might be fun. She had changed and he had waited in the hotel bar, had the good sense to drink a Coke. When she came into the bar he wanted to say she looked beautiful, didn't say anything at all.

Easy come, easy go. She'd been to places, making films, talking to people, Serbia and Kosovo and Greece, places from the news, and it surprised him how much someone might know and not know. She spoke some Russian, had said things to him in it, and how would someone go about learning Russian? Maybe clever people were always naive.

'This place will be rougher than it looks,' he said. And he said it as a joke, because it didn't look much from the outside. They stepped around a puddle of smashed glass. He realized when they parked up that it was an old factory social club. The factory had long gone. There were orange houses built on what had been the football ground and bowls club behind it. He had a vague recollection of once being here with his dad. She slipped her arm into his and said, 'You'd better look after me, then.' He could feel her body against his and her hair against his cheek.

There were stone leopards on either side of the doors and a big man in white gloves standing inside the entrance to take their coats and usher them to their seats. The place was not full, a couple of big groups laughing and all talking at once, clinking glasses, people done up for a night out. There were tables with kids eating ice cream, a few couples leaning towards each other across their food. Candles flickered in the golden fittings. He breathed a bit more easily, recognized the elephants at the top of the stairs, and the wooden screens and lamps. He put his hand on the broad forehead of one of the elephants, the wood was cool to the touch. He saw the waiter look at him, Grace too.

'This used to be somewhere else,' he said, by way of explanation. And it had, in a place in Dudley where he used to go with Natalie, but which had closed down, done out with carved elephants and water features much like this place, and that was like the Jamie he remembered, big on ideas, but never his own. And they walked through the restaurant alongside the narrow canal that crossed the floor and wound between the tables back to a central fountain. There was the sound and sparkle of tumbling water. There were koi carp swimming by their feet.

'This place is incredible,' she said. 'I love it.'

And she did, because there was something she wanted to say to him, about how for all his talk of loss and defeat there were people having a good time here, making the most of things, getting on with life. The zoo animals in the middle of the town, riding on the Ferris wheel, the sound of laughter: that was the story as well, she wanted to say. It wasn't everyone or everything that was sinking, it seemed to her, not like the way he described it. The truth was that the people she'd spoken to, with the exception of Cairo, had said they were voting to give things a go, that the country would be fine on its own in the world. Even Cairo's dad had said that, after a fashion. People shrugged their shoulders and said it was no big deal. Grace had learned to think that this was delusional, held back from saying so in the interviews, but was not quite as sure as she had been. She thought of her mother muttering at the television news, was struck by something Cairo had said to her: 'Has it ever occurred to you that you might be wrong?' She was not convinced it ever had.

Cairo said he had never been one for spicy food after the waiter got their orders the wrong way round. She worried momentarily that this would wound him, wondered why it bothered her, as he pulled carefully at the naan bread, looked at the dishes between them.

Some hair had tumbled out of her clip and fallen onto her neck, and he looked at her and it seemed to say something about her. That there was some carelessness to her, he thought, that if you had so much going for you, you could afford to be careless. She looked over to a table that she said must be the UKIP people, though how she could tell was beyond him. He looked at the way her hair fell against her neck, wanted to touch her hair, her neck.

Which is how the fight came to surprise him. There was a shout from a few tables away, from behind one of the wooden screens that partitioned the space, the smash of glass and a woman's scream, the sound of things overturned. Two men crashed through the screen and grappled and tumbled half into the water. A carp brushed the ear of the man on the bottom. The man on top had a tear in the shoulder of his suit jacket, a trickle of blood ran from behind his ear. They breathed heavily, humped each other across the floor, half in and half out of the water. Cairo sensed the fight had already blown itself out, he heard one of the men grunt, 'Enough,' although whether as statement or question he wasn't sure.

The waiters were running now, the big man from the door too, tearing off his white gloves, and the men grappled slowly, their upset table some way behind them, and wives and girlfriends and brothers and mates stood with their hands to their mouths in shock, silver balloons with the number 40 printed on them hung suspended in the air around them. The two men had been eating together. And it looked like that would be it, some kind of minor diversion, entertainment, and that the men would dust themselves down in the car park outside and perhaps even resume their night out, something to laugh off tomorrow afternoon in the pub, when the big man from the door, the waiters buoyed and cocky in his presence, came and hauled the bloke on top that bit too aggressively, and Cairo saw he gave him a little dig to the kidneys as he raised him, and who could blame him really, but his family and mates all saw too, their table upset, their food and the night going to ruin, and that was when it all kicked off.

One of the men who had stood at the upset table came to life, his glasses askew on his red face, bent and picked up an already broken pint glass and hurled it at the bouncer. It was a wild throw, missed by a good few feet and shattered against the wall by which Cairo and Grace sat. Cairo felt a couple of chips of glass hit him, reached across the table, touched Grace's arm and motioned for her to get down, hemmed in as they were, actually put his hand on top of her head, but she manoeuvred herself out of the way, and everyone in the restaurant stood or ducked below the tables or made a run for it. Cairo saw a family of four, young boys in matching shirts, one holding an ice cream like an injured bird, scramble up the steps to the exit doors. There was the sound of more breaking glass.

The men who had started the fight were already halfway to the doors, harried by waiters and chefs, who appeared from nowhere. A man in stained white kitchen

clothes waved a heavy rolling pin. Cairo wondered if
he'd go back and fetch a knife. One of the wooden
elephants tottered and crashed on its side. The people
from the table followed, as if in a carnival procession,
men and women both throwing punches now, at each
other, at the waiters.

A man stumbled, came crashing towards Cairo and
Grace's table, the man who had thrown the glass, he was
sure, but with no glasses on his face, possibly the man's
brother. There was a tablecloth somehow tucked into the
man's belt, so he dragged upset curries and pickles that
bled across the white material behind him. He blundered
wildly at Cairo, windmilled his arms, so Cairo punched
him, instinctively the first time, and when the man did
not go to ground, but waved his arms even more wildly
in front of him, punched him a second time, with more
purpose, and it wasn't a great connection, but the bloke
went back the way he came anyway, treading through the
food that he'd strewn behind him, splashing korma and
rogan josh up his trousers and across the room before
he went down onto the floor, from where two waiters
dragged him towards the door.

And then it was over as suddenly as it had begun and
everything went quiet. The sounds of flowing water
and sitar music came back. There was a shout from out
in the car park, and then another, and the waiters and
kitchen staff came back in through the doors and started
righting chairs and tables, sweeping up glass, people
at half a dozen separate tables sat down or re-emerged

and dusted themselves off and all tried to decide what to do.

'Wow!' Grace said, a bit breathless. 'I didn't expect that. Are you OK?'

'I'm all right,' he said, a bit indignant at the calm way she spoke, expected she'd be a bit more shaken, wished she was.

She put her hand to her hair and picked something out. He wrung his right hand, could feel it starting to swell, had done something to it with that bad connection.

Jamie Iqbal moved between the tables in his expensive suit and tried to reassure people who were getting up to leave. When he reached Cairo, he held out his hand to shake, and Cairo had to offer him his left. 'I thought you'd died,' Jamie said, 'it's been so long.'

Jamie moved them to a table by the bar, joined them for a drink, brought them brandies and a couple of slices of cake while the waiters continued to right the chairs and lay out new tablecloths, and the UKIP meeting, which had indeed been the table Grace identified, handed out leaflets to the people who had stayed. A woman nodded enthusiastically at something another woman said to her.

'There'll be none of that kind of thing if we leave the EU,' Grace said as a joke that neither Jamie nor Cairo acknowledged. Then, getting drunk, she told them a story of being in a bar somewhere in Serbia once, and a fight had broken out and the barman fired his gun into the ceiling, and Jamie and Cairo had looked suitably impressed, Cairo with his hand in a bucket of ice.

Cairo nearly told Jamie he wanted to fight again, right there, it was where the idea came to him. Jamie said he'd book them a car when they were ready, raised an eyebrow when Cairo said he was driving but said nothing else, apologized again for the trouble, shook his head at any offer of them paying, said, 'Fuckers who cor hold their drink,' then apologized for his bad language to Grace. 'One minute we was about to fetch the birthday cake out, next minute all hell breaks loose. Fuckers from Brierley Hill. Some family feud erupted, just like that.'

'Like they do,' said Cairo.

'Like they do,' said Jamie.

And all the time Cairo was talking to Jamie, he could feel Grace looking at him, and he put his good hand on the table, and for a long time it seemed like their hands stayed there next to each other, and then their hands touched and Grace put her hand on his, and he didn't look at her, could sense her looking at him, and felt her hand resting there.

'Well, you look like you can still handle yerself, Cairo,' Jamie said. 'You take care, you hear that, mate. Try to make it less than a decade next time, eh?'

When Jamie left they moved their hands. Cairo said he was sorry and Grace said he had nothing to apologize for at all.

He rested his swollen right hand on top of the steering wheel, drove as best he could with that and the drink.

They had the windows open and the fresh air helped him, the smell of flowers and exhaust fumes in the car. There was that sweet, sickly smell that came from the brewery on the wind when he was a kid. The brewery had gone, of course. They were nearly at the hotel, slowing down at the bottom of Castle Hill, and he intended to say something about the old train station, long since shut, thought to mention the flowers planted on the roundabout, EU-funded, when blue lights shone enormous through the back window. He saw the police car in the wing mirror. He felt his stomach turn, pulled over onto the track that ran down the side of the zoo, towards the old freight depot, decided he might tell them straight away about his licence, no point in letting them work it out for themselves. There was that and the drink. There was a burst of the siren and the traffic went haphazard at the lights, cars pulled up at strange angles to the white lines. The police car pulled alongside them – Cairo could see a young policewoman talking, she glanced at Cairo – and then it went for a gap in the stopped traffic, the siren blaring again now, and raced off towards the Wolverhampton Road. It took him a moment to realize that they were in the clear. He sighed, had been holding his breath.

'We should have got a cab, Cairo. I wouldn't want to get you into trouble, for you to feel you had to drive me around.' Her voice broke calmly through the dark.

'Yer day force the drink down me neck,' he said, was aware of his accent as he said it, became aware that he had been softening it, of course he had, for her, not even fully conscious of this until now, and also thinking that it was good to say something about the drink, not to mention the licence. Without the car she wouldn't be here.

'Take your time,' she said.

The lights of the traffic illuminated their faces and he wondered if something might happen right here in the car, both of them aware of the other sitting in the half-dark. But then nothing happened, they sat in the car with the lights of the hotel visible across the lanes of traffic ahead and he did not want the night to finish yet.

'I wanna show you something,' he said, easing the car onto the track between a crumbling wall and a fence.

'What's down here?' she said, a hint of concern in her voice which he didn't mind at all. It made him feel good. Back in control. He'd protect her. He turned off the car headlights and the track ran into the dark as if into the hill itself.

'Elephant bones,' he said.

She'd mentioned the caves earlier, how she'd been to the new visitor centre on the canal and filmed the narrow-boats in the sunshine. He told her about the miles of tunnels down there, prohibited, unexplored, that they used to try to break into them as kids, told her a long rambling story about a bloke hiding down there years ago with a gun, some kind of siege. Sieges were his kind of thing, she knew that much already.

She was glad of the fresh air, told herself she wasn't drunk. He opened the car boot and fumbled in it in the dark and with his bad hand, swore quietly, and she wondered for a moment about the clank of metal and what he might turn from the car with in his hands and how she did not know this man at all, not really, suddenly illuminated in a pool of light from the torch he held. He held a second torch out to her, which she took, and looked at rope and old rags and wood and lengths of chain strewn in the back of the car, the stuff of his work, she supposed, but it gave her a shiver.

'There was a time when they'd sling the dead animals from the zoo down here in an old pit.'

Some way down the path there was a hole in the fence. There was a sign up of a guard dog but they heard no dogs, nothing, along the path that ran alongside what seemed like a cliff. They were somewhere under the castle. There were the grooves of old railway lines along the path.

'Longer we stand here, the more chance of getting caught,' he said, and he stepped through the gap.

'Where are we going?' she said. 'What are we looking for?'

'Elephant bones,' he said again, and he shone the torch against the wall in front of them and the dark of an opening in the rock like something from a fairy tale.

'Here we go,' he said. The torches zigzagged across a curve in the tunnel wall and they walked into the side of the hill.

'Slow,' he said.

She looked at the rough stone floor in the two beams of torchlight, imagined strange creatures at the edge of the light. The floor disappeared and Cairo put his arm out to stop her. 'Slow,' he said again. 'This is it.'

They crept forward to the edge of the hole in front of them, held the torches out over the rim. A long way below she could see something heaped, the texture of a shingle beach, could be bones. A beach made of bones, water down there too, there was something cool and damp in the air that rose from the hole.

'They threw an elephant down here once,' he said. 'It had died at the zoo and no one knew how to get rid of it. The town was plagued with bluebottles that whole summer. It's still there, I think. Tony will send us down for the ivory one day, I swear, when we've dug everything else up.'

He turned his torch off. There was the light from her torch in the pit below them. It was not as dark as she would have imagined, buried in a hill.

'Look up,' he said. The top of the shaft opened to the night sky. Shapes flickered across the area of lighter dark that was the sky. There was a faint squeaking sound. 'Bats,' he said.

They stayed there for a while, on the edge of the collapsed hole, on the floor of the tunnel, looking up at the sky. A light blinked and for a moment she thought it was a star, but then saw it was a banking plane. Beautiful nonetheless.

He said to keep the torches low as they walked back, in case of security doing the rounds. He'd told her that in the war there had been a plan to put a whole munitions factory in the tunnels under the castle, that there was a shadow town under the real one, the whole place meshed with bones, fossils, zoo animals, plague and cholera pits. It seemed important to him, the idea that not everything could be seen. That there was some truth out of reach of filming or reason.

Back near the tunnel mouth, they heard car wheels on the path, saw headlights illuminate the walls for a moment and then move away. The car seemed very near, and the engine echoed in the tunnel, then it passed, and the rumble of it stayed, and the sound of it going away again. They stood close together while they waited for the car to pass, their torches switched off. When they were sure the car had gone they went to move and bumped into each other, half by accident, their faces close in the dark, and then they kissed, hidden there inside the tunnel for a while, leaning against the wall where the surface changed from concrete to limestone.

After

There's something gone wrong with his mother's tablets and Cairo watches her, dizzy and bad-tempered as she bends to the oven door, warming the plates for his old man to get back from the chip shop. Cairo had said he'd go back out, but his dad took it as an insult. He said he'd do the plates too but she motioned for him to sit down.

They miss the dog, it's one of the times of day his dad used to take him out. They said they wouldn't have another, said it would be too much after Titan died, and regret that now, but can't have one with Stacey-Ann and the baby here. Stacey-Ann butters the bread, waits for the baby's bottle to warm, and his mother looks over her shoulder. She's doing OK is what Cairo wants to say to her, stop mithering.

His dad rattles the back door and stands on the mat to take off his jacket. Stacey-Ann unwraps the fish and chips, a doner for her, and they step around each other, too many people in the room, to the kitchen table.

'I cor eat that, I cor, our Stacey-Ann.' His dad jabs his knife across the table at the grey meat that lies across Stacey-Ann's chips.

'I ay askin yer to, Grandad,' Stacey-Ann says.

'Yer doh know what they put in it, yer doh.'

'I like it,' she says.

Cairo stands at the grill, turns his chicken breasts over with a fork. He'd bought a pack of frozen chicken, in the belief that work would be regular for a bit longer, had counted on being paid a full week. The beans bubble in the saucepan, and that and the smell of the chips that fills the room now make him hungry. He wills the chicken to cook under the blue flame.

'Nice fish, Nan?' Stacey-Ann says.

'Iss all right,' his mother says. The girl deserves a medal for her cheerfulness.

He dishes up his chicken and beans on one of the warmed plates, eases into the chair next to Stacey-Ann. He can see through the door to the baby who lies on his play mat. The boy's fist paws at a soft teddy bear that hangs suspended above him. He catches it a blow and gurgles contentedly. Something eases in Cairo for a moment. He tries a mouthful of beans, too hot.

'Yow in training?' His dad jabs his knife again, towards Cairo's plate this time, something accusatory, mocking, is what he hears in the tone.

'What? No, what yer on about?'

'What with that and the running.'

'No, just fancied summat different. I've gorra try and keep in a bit of shape wi the work.'

His old man looks at him across the table.

'Iss too much for yer now, Cairo, that work. He'll work yer to jeth, that bloody Clancey. They'm all the same,' his mother says, and shakes her head.

'What, the Clanceys? Half of em never done a bloody day's work in their life.' His dad sounds like he's having a row even when he asks if anyone wants a cup of tea. With talk of the Clanceys, he looks like he might kill someone. He continues to jab his fork in the air.

'The gaffers, I mean. The gaffers am all the same,' his mom says.

'I doh know what else yow expect me to do, Mother.'

'Yome hard worker, I know that, love. They tek advantage of yer.'

The way she says this, something about the light falling into the kitchen and the way he sits in a different chair to usual so that he watches her side on, and can see her work her new teeth off her lower jaw and then back on again, and look somewhere over the sink as if she is blind and merely senses the presence of her family somewhere near, moves him. Get through a day at a time, that's what people did, he knew that. There were people here in front of him doing exactly that.

It is hot in the kitchen now, their food almost gone. His dad smears a last round of bread across his plate and leans back in his chair.

'I'll put the kettle on, before we go,' Stacey-Ann says. 'D'yer want to give Zach his bottle, Dad?'

'Goo on, then,' Cairo says, wishes he could say more, something like, of course I do, I'd love to. He picks the boy up, holds him, remembers for a moment how he did this with Stacey-Ann. And he sees again that other baby that will not be. Blood and remains, like something the fox might nose through. Is the horror in the world or in his head, or both? 'What to do about it,' is what she said.

Once, not long after Stacey-Ann was born, he'd fought down in London, stepped in at the last minute on the undercard of a Howard Eastman fight, because they knew he'd give them value even with taking a fight at the last minute, and they'd stayed in a hotel afterwards. Both his eyes had been shut from the fight, closed to slits, and they'd worried about the baby, Stacey-Ann, seeing them, and he remembers that she hadn't cried and he'd laid her on his chest, propped up on the bed, and she'd touched his closed eyes gently with her fingertips and then settled down to sleep.

He remembers Natalie moving silently around the hotel bedroom, the biggest room they had ever slept in. She was wearing a silk dressing gown that he'd bought her to wear in the hospital after having Stacey-Ann. They had been kids, really. What would he have been then, twenty-three? Nat was only twenty. Maybe they were kids, but it seems to him that he had more idea of who he was then. He'd fought that Welsh boy, Iolo Farr, who they made out was a relation of Tommy Farr to build some story up around him, talking him up as the next big thing. They'd gone the distance, and the kid had closed both of Cairo's eyes but couldn't finish him off, and he didn't amount to anything much in the end, faded away soon after. That was a fight Cairo might have won, he realizes now, years too late, and his life might have taken a different course. Natalie kissed his closed eyes while Stacey-Ann slept on his chest. They had some money in the bank. Not enough. She walked out not long after her twenty-first birthday. Natalie is doing fine now. Stacey-Ann tries not to say too much. When she was younger they'd sit in the McDonald's, or in the window in the Beatties café, and she'd complain endlessly about her mother and he'd find himself defending Nat to her. Natalie could look after herself, of that he has always been certain. She lent him that money to tide him over, without Tony knowing, charged him interest.

The kettle boils.

'You having tea, Dad?'

He nods. 'Where am yer going anyway?' he asks her.

Before

'You have no tattoos,' she said to him, a week or so after they kissed, the day he took the dressing off his hand.

She had a tattoo. Two, in fact. Small ones, a Cornish knot on her right ankle, a small dolphin above her left wrist.

'You've given yourself hands for radio,' her mother said in the kitchen when Grace pulled back the bandage, and cried.

He smiled and said, 'What did you expect? Some big eagle across me chest?' He kissed the dolphin. She found them silly, embarrassing, the tattoos, her ankle more so than her wrist, although that was daft enough, which she got not long after her dad died and had hurt much more, the needle right against the bone, and she had wanted the pain, she supposed. The dolphin she got with her sister, when Esther had been old enough to know better and Grace not, according to their mother, when Grace was a student, back for the holidays, wandering around Camden Lock like they had done as kids, pretending it was Ibiza, that they were some lost children of the raves, rather than home on vacation from Lady Margaret Hall.

'I could get an old work scene,' Cairo said. 'Some bloke bashing metal, by the canal, the castle in the distance. The myth of the Black Country worker. You could film it.'

That view is exactly what they filmed one morning. She tried to get him to say what he had in the interview in the hotel lounge in Dudley but it didn't come out right. The view was exactly right: rusting metal and overhanging trees, and the castle indeed in the distance.

After a while, he said, 'Does that disappoint yer? No tattoos. Not authentic enough.' But he was still smiling.

'No, of course not,' she said. 'I regret having these done now. They don't seem to belong to me.'

'I might have considered one. You know, when Stacey-Ann was born, her name or date of birth or summat. I cor stand the idea of the needle.'

'Like it was someone else, another person altogether who got them done. The dolphin was my sister's idea.'

'Or like Tyson's one of Arthur Ashe. You know, the tennis player. *Days of Grace*, it says.'

'People change, I suppose, that might be a reason to have one, to remind yourself of who you once were.'

'Or a reason not to have one,' he said.

She had not thought he was listening, and his suggestion pleased her more than she believed it should.

'Days of Grace,' he said again.

When she got together with Anwar, she had wondered about something in Arabic, high on her leg, out of sight, except for him. Of course, he was not a man so keen on tattoos either. Cairo put his hands on her shoulders, moved his thumbs into the muscle there.

'That's nice,' she said, eased back into him. 'That's it.'

She had mentioned her shoulder ached from the bag and the camera. He said when he finished boxing massage was one of the things he'd considered doing, said he used to get a rub-down after fights, after training, get the knots out of his muscles. She wanted to say that he was a strange and beautiful man. The sun came in through a gap in the curtains, moved slowly across the room.

Later, there was the sun in the room and not much else, the ebb and flow of traffic through the window, a sound that always seemed near here, often the sound of tyres on wet concrete after rain, the sound of people going somewhere else. The sun sliced across the bed. Hopper crossed her mind. And that she was becoming the woman in one of those paintings, looking towards the window at nothing in particular. A woman sitting in a pattern of sunlight in a hotel room after a man has gone. The feeling that she had done this before nagged at her. And it was true that she'd had that brief romance – yes, why not call it that? – with Marko, the fixer in Belgrade, and she had sat in a grander hotel room than this, under chandeliers, listening to distant traffic in a city and a country that considered itself cursed, and may have had a point.

After

No one speaks for a moment, they look at each other across the last of the chips. He knows what's coming before she says it.

'I spoke to me mom,' is what she says, doesn't look at him, considers her empty plate, pushes a piece of bread at a smear of brown sauce.

'What did her have to say for herself, then?'

'Asked if I wanted to go back.'

'Did her apologize to yer?'

'Her said we'd find a new way of doing things.'

'But her day apologize to yer.'

Stacey-Ann is still wiping at her plate with her bread. *We'll find a new way of doing things*, it's what her mother had scrawled in the letter, no apology, and it's like her dad can see through it. They have not actually spoken. Stacey-Ann texted Tony when she read the letter. Her shoulders are hunched, like she's in some slow-motion flinch, as if he would do anything more than speak to her in this low, even voice. As if he ever has. His parents have moved their chairs back away from the table, looking at least as if they would like to disappear. He is thankful for that.

'A woman who threw her own daughter and grandson out on the street. Who wanted her own grandson gone.'

'Her asked me if I wanted to come back.'

'You could say no.'

Zach starts to cry from the front room.

'He's hungry, Stacey-Ann,' his mother says.

'Yer still want to feed him, Dad?' Stacey-Ann says, tries to sound cheerful, gets up from the chair to get the bottle.

Cairo doesn't say anything, rises, and walks through into the front room, puts his hand down to the baby, who cries even harder. He feels Stacey-Ann enter the room behind him. This house is too small, is one of the things she might say to him if he forced her to say more, but it isn't, and he walks to the foot of the stairs. He can see her case, Zach's changing bag, a couple of carrier bags. He had come in the back door, of course, and she would have known he would. If they hadn't finished work early he wouldn't have seen them at all.

He takes the boy in his arms and sits in the armchair by the window, holds Zach tightly as he gulps at the milk. He kisses the top of the boy's head. Zach balls his little fist. Aims a punch at his grandad's chin and Cairo smiles at him.

'He's a lovely boy,' Cairo says.

'I'll come round tomorrow as normal, Dad?'

She says this as if it's a question. Back to the Saturday routine they've had since she was a girl. He feels the urge to see if she wants to go to the pictures, bowling, wants the years to turn back. They can walk over the park with Zach in the pram.

'Of course,' Cairo says.

A horn sounds from outside. He can see there is a car pulled up on the other side of the hedge, knows full well who it is.

'Did yer book a taxi?' he asks.

'No,' she says. 'Tony said he'd come and pick me up.'

'Of course he did.'

He overheard her once, years ago, when she was still a young girl, twelve, thirteen or so, they were here late on a Saturday night, he remembers. She was on the phone, he was late for getting back to her mother. He heard Stacey-Ann say dad and he thought she was talking to him, went to the bedroom door, his bedroom when he was a boy, his bedroom now, and said her name.

She was talking, still talking on the phone, and he heard her say dad again down the phone, no idea that she could call him that, she always said Tony to him. He had felt something slip inside himself. He crept down the stairs and said, 'All right love?' when she emerged.

Stacey-Ann stands at the front door with Zach. Cairo wants to help her with her bags but can't face Tony.

'I'll see you tomorrow, darling,' he says, kisses her cheek, touches Zach's face. His mom goes to the front step. He sits down again, listens to Tony turning the car around in the narrow street, hopes he scratches it on the rose bushes that overhang the wall.

Before

She was never late, and it was on her mind that it was possible. She even felt sick one morning when she had got up with the intention of heading to the ponds and instead had to lie back down and watch the trees for a while, and her head feeling so heavy and surely, surely you could not feel it that quickly. And she did not know how she felt, how to feel about the prospect at all. She had always wanted a child and with Anwar, it was he who had said to wait, they had argued about it, in the weeks after her thirtieth birthday, such a cliché. She could never understand whether that was what began to open up the divide between them or whether that tension simply exposed existing fault lines. It didn't matter in the end, she supposed.

She was busy in these June weeks. She tried to bury that feeling first thing in the morning, the dizziness if she turned in the pool, the heaviness of her head in the afternoon, wanted to ask her sister, 'Was it like this for you?' Held her tongue. One reason she had begun to spend time with her sister again was friends with babies. They had them all at the same time like some kind of epidemic. When she refused a glass of wine from Esther, her sister raised an eyebrow, said, 'You haven't got something to tell us, Grace?' as a joke, and when she answered too quickly and blushed, she saw her mother raise her eyes from the *New Yorker* to look at her for a moment and say nothing.

So it was the morning of the 23rd, a couple of weeks late now, and the feeling of heaviness still with her, that she bought two kits at Euston station, the girl on the till smiling at her hopefully, might as well have given her a thumbs up, and pregnant women everywhere, across the concourse with their great bellies, and babies in carriers and those papoose things that she was sure everyone would assume she would want to wear if she were to have a baby, if she were to have this baby. It had reached the point where she'd be disappointed if the test said no.

She was getting the train to Sandwell and Dudley station, which was not in Dudley at all, it turned out. Franco was with her to take some shots at the polling stations. On the train that swayed and made her feel even more sick, she peed all over her hand as well as the test thing somewhere past Milton Keynes, and she looked at the thick blue lines on the tester and felt, curiously, not much at all, too hot, a bit woozy. She wondered if it was shock, a bit much to take in, and texted Cairo to say she was filming and to let her know if he was around today, and what to say to him, what to say?

After

He lies on the bed, tired, shouldn't be this tired. All of them the same. He hopes his mother has a sleep this afternoon. Tiredness has worked through everything, like the damp that warps the walls and the back fence and the wallpaper in the bathroom, has worked its way through the hills themselves, the undermining of the tunnels and great caverns that shift below them, slowly, not in human time, bent everything out of shape in the end. But the tiredness is human, that much is certain, and the damage done.

He pictures a route up the hill, tries to concentrate on something else. Sunday mornings he would run up over the hill, along Oakham Road, try not look up towards Tony and Natalie's house, a glance up the drive at the fancy cars, a glance up at the window he thought was Stacey-Ann's room, lengthen his stride, the warrior. They could keep their cars and their fancy house. They would all one day be dust. He stopped often by the horses in the field a little way off the road from there. Up past the

Hangman's Tree. The hangman had come from a farm near here. Thousands would attend and watch him go about his business. They put wooden grandstands up once all along the road to Stafford jail so the crowds could see the scaffold and the hangman wrestling with the dangling, dancing figure on the rope. Cairo would spit onto the path churned with horseshoe patterns. The horses would snort in the field, one might break into a gallop. You might see the riders coming down the path and the horses would breathe and stamp in the field and he could never work out if they were happy to go out or if it was fear. Fear of pale young women in their hats and boots, with their whips.

And Cairo would bolt down the hill, racing the water that ran off and ended up in the Severn, down and over the Rowley Road and through Warren's Hall and past the ponds and the gravel where they used to sometimes torch the cars and down the black paths, past the ruin of the engine house where the engine had pumped water from the mines, and the coal had fired the engines and the furnaces, and forged the country as it became. And here were the ruins, and here were the ghost people among them, lost tribes, fields of bones, that the people who had done so well from it all now wanted gone, erased. Not one reminder of where they had come from was to stay.

People are tired. Tired of clammed-up factory gates, but not even them any more, because look where they are working now, digging trenches to tat out the last of whatever metal was left. Tired of change, tired of the world passing by, tired of other people getting things that you and people like you had made for them, tired of being told you were no good, tired of being told that what you believed to be true was wrong, tired of being told to stop complaining, tired of being told what to eat, what to throw away, what to do and what not to do, what was right and wrong when you were always in the wrong. Tired of supermarket jobs and warehouse jobs and jobs guarding shopping centres. Work had always worn people out, the heat of furnaces, the clang of iron, but this is tiredness of a different order, tiredness that a rest will not cure, like a plague, eating away at them all.

He wants to close his eyes, with his feet off the end of the bed he slept in as a child, with nothing but the sound of the house creaking and settling, and the shush of the traffic like the tide on a distant shore and the murmur of the telly from downstairs. Tiredness like ash in your mouth.

'What to do about it.' That was what she had said on the message, the last one, repeated what she'd said when they'd rowed on the towpath. They were the words that Natalie had used too, when she told him about Stacey-Ann being pregnant. What to do about it. A human life. A new life. But Stacey-Ann was stubborn, at least, and the boy too, Zachariah, would cling to life, you could see that. That his grandmother wanted him gone, cut away, was something he could never know.

To start again anew: the only cure for this tiredness. To leave our old selves behind and become someone new.

And babies could do that, children, they were someone new without all the old tiredness. But not for long, he supposed. What to do about it. He knows full well what she means. She's probably done it by now.

They dump the dead babies in wheelie bins when they've cut them out. He saw it in the paper once. They were sheltering out of the rain somewhere. Tony had treated them to a breakfast and he looked over at one of the blokes reading the paper and there was a story about the babies being found in a bin out the back of a clinic. Not a backstreet place. A clinic in London. Not even bodies, parts of bodies he supposed, half-formed things, but flesh and blood. What to do about it, is what Natalie said, tried to persuade Stacey-Ann to get rid of the baby. It, they called it. Soft bones like jelly, sticky on the side of the bin. They cut them out. Or suck them out with something like a Hoover. He'd read that too. Had to get up from his breakfast, stood out and looked at the rain falling in the street.

'Yow all right?' Luke asked him. 'Yome like a ghost. Al's ating yer breakfast.'

'I'm all right,' he said. 'I'm all right.'

He closes his eyes and sees bones bursting up out of the field below the churchyard. Sees the bones come with a life of their own, dancing through the streets. Sees the wheelie-bin lid rattle. Translucent tiny hands, curled pale bodies with little black-spot eyes, reaching out, crying out. Buckets of blood and flesh. They are monsters, these fucking people. It was strange, because

Natalie had used those words to him. 'What to do about it. What to do about the baby.'

'Like, what do you mean, what to do about it?' he'd said. It was as if he could see straight through her flesh, saw her jawbone as she said the words, the sockets for her eyes. As if he was talking to a skeleton, to a ghost.

'What to do about it,' she'd said again in her posh voice on her phone message.

'Hello, Cairo. It's Grace,' she said, and he swears to God that he felt something lift in him, something move in him. Her voice, that she had phoned, and it might still all come good. He swears to himself that the sun glimmered briefly on the cut as he heard it, and that feeling must have lasted – what? – seconds. He was stood there, looking at the water, the wobbly sense of himself, and the message ended and there was another, with her voice rougher at the edges and then this last one, like she had a cold, but he realizes she must have been crying, which was to her credit, he supposes, not the chance of a tear had he seen in Natalie's eye when she came with her what to do about it. Like we had the say over life and death. A few seconds. The sun went in again, grey water, the colour of ash. He could never tell anyone that. Who would there be to tell? The kind of thing you might tell a woman like her if you got to spend time with her. You could say: There was sun on the water. And she'd know what you meant.

But it was people like them who should be cut out, dumped in pits or bins, left to rot at the side of the road and let the crows pick them clean. Here was the anger come now, concussive episodes was a phrase they'd used, a man getting bashed in the head to put food on the table, to pay the rent. Natalie left him because she wanted to buy a house. Of course she did. It was the boxers who lived like monks he always admired, not those with the cars and the clothes, the gold teeth, the tigers on leads. Those who ran and trained quietly in the woods, would sleep in a cave if they could, drink water from streams. Live with purity, simplicity. He knew these were sometimes the same people, men drawn to excess of all kinds.

Before

They held hands, walking by the canal. The day was less busy than Grace had planned. She got the images of people queuing at a polling station, Franco was already on a train back to London.

Sometimes a heron was waiting on the bank on the other side, Cairo told her, but he hadn't seen it for a while. He then told her how he'd legged it through a tunnel once, years ago, they let you do it at the museum. It was what they had to do in the barges before they made tunnels big enough for horses to get down. You would roll onto your back and put your feet on the tunnel roof, so low above you and the boat and the water, and walk across the bricks, push the barge onwards.

'We should do it one time,' is what he said. The tone in his voice and this picture of them lying side by side, as they walked now hand in hand by the water, no one else around, made her tell him.

She told him she wasn't sure at first, she might just be late, of course it was possible. But she'd done the tests with two kits, she told him. And she'd booked a doctor's appointment for next week.

He was calm as she said these things, she would swear now, like she had somehow remembered it all wrong. His face was calm and he nodded, had turned towards her. Were they still holding hands?

She said something like how they would need to decide what to do about it.

'What do you mean, what to do about it?'

'Well, I mean what to do.' She still was not sure that this was anger. Uncertainty, yes. She realized now that she'd hoped he would say that's wonderful and hold her in his arms, in spite of whatever difficulties that might come. How difficult could it be? They were adults, neither of them in a relationship.

'What?'

'Well, I don't know.'

'You do know, what to do about it.'

'What's the matter?'

'You said what to do about it?'

Anger, hatred, fear in his eyes, she could see. She was aware that her back was to the water, the narrow canal towpath. The distant sound of traffic from the top of the embankment.

'I didn't think you'd be like this, please.'

'Iss easy for people like you. What to do about it? What, have you done this kind of thing before?'

'What are you talking about?'

He did raise his hands. This might be the only thing

they would both agree on later, not that there was a later where they sat down to discuss matters. He raised his hands towards her, to do what? Hold her, stop her?

'What to do about it.'

He'd pushed her, or maybe he'd pushed her, his hands were on her, and it happened so fast that she wasn't so sure afterwards. She struggled. Her back was to the wall now. Better the wall, not the water, otherwise she might go in. She saw his face, the anger in it. They were alone on the towpath and she didn't know him, not really, not at all. She had come here looking for something. Found something, well enough.

He was swearing, she wasn't sure what he was saying. He blocked her path and she was scared. She turned to run back the way she'd come, up the steps to the road, she had the minicab number in her phone, could see the hotel across an empty factory site, lanes of traffic, the castle up there on the hill. He didn't come after her.

She could hear him on the towpath shouting, 'Grace, Grace, Grace,' the words getting further away in the traffic.

Later, she phoned him, left a message, then another, no word from him at all.

The doctor, a locum, didn't say much, no questions, no congratulations, nothing, only to decide on a hospital. That the birthing centre was in the same building as the ward seemed a good idea to the doctor. She'd get a letter about a scan.

She thought of the girl, Ann, in the clinic. 'I don't really see his dad,' she'd said, 'but I wouldn't change it, wouldn't change him,' and for a moment she was not sure if she meant the baby or the father.

She phoned every few days, got a dead tone.

She even went to vote that night, when she got back. In part, to placate her mother, who texted when she was on the train asking if she had been to vote before she left. So she dragged herself up the hill to the primary school she had attended as a girl, even though she was so tired she wanted to sit down on the kerb outside the gates, and would have if she hadn't been cutting it so fine to make it in time, pointless as it was, the result preordained, and she would have gladly missed it except that it wasn't worth the aggravation from her mother.

In the booth she leaned on the little shelf, almost closed her eyes, could have gone to sleep right there. When voting she often became paranoid she'd put her cross in the wrong box. She looked at the ballot paper now, held the pencil in her hand, looked at the black lines on the paper. After a while she put the pencil down, folded the paper, walked out across the schoolroom and dropped it unmarked into the box.

She did sit on the kerb, bought a carton of orange juice and a packet of Monster Munch from the shop, the snack she used to buy from the same shop as a young girl. The clink of glasses and the sound of voices and laughter rose from the pub garden into the darkening sky. The sound of someone playing a piano came from one of the houses. She sat on the kerb and listened to the piano and the swish of cycle tyres on the road and the babble of voices from the pub. She would walk home in a moment, sleep through well into the morning, awake in another country.

After

Grace looks out of the window here at the café, sees Franco come along the road, checking his phone. There are boys stood round a bike on the corner looking at him. He carries his camera in a bag on his shoulder, equipment in another backpack. His clothes are a nondescript black, his hair is dark and falls half across his face and he sometimes ties it back when he is filming, but he is not ostentatious, should not stand out, but he does, somehow. She can see the boys watching him. And at first she can't identify what is so different. The equipment? The bags? He squints at the café sign. Confidence. Privilege.

A group of men turn at the corner, go up the steps of the pub. She sees one of them look back at Franco, hitch his trousers, say something to the younger man next to him, who laughs. The man with the eye, she is sure she has seen him before, he was with Cairo that first day, when she was asking people to talk. Ally or Alan, something like that. She wants to get up and cross the street and call him back, that was the man who swore at her, told her to go back where she belonged. The possibility that Cairo might be with them rises in her and her hand shakes, she can see it against the plastic tabletop.

'This place is a hole,' Franco says to her, and sits down.

'I've never heard you say that anywhere. Hungary, the border camps, Serbia, when you came back from Syria. Never. But Dudley is the end of the road for you. Look out of the window. It's a sunny afternoon in the English Midlands.'

Franco is thrown for a moment, has never heard cynicism, anger, in her voice before.

'Those places have got an excuse, a reason for being how they are, but these people,' Franco says.

'Ah, these people,' she says, 'these people. There is them and us. These fucking people.'

She takes the headphones plug from the socket. Turns the volume low but beckons for him to lean in and listen. There is Cairo's face on the screen.

'A lot of it is gone, erased. The industrial past. And a lot of it is hidden away. The point is the people here built the country as it was to become. Now you act – we act – like there's some sort of shame to it all. The rest of the country is ashamed of us. You want us gone in one way or the other. It'll end in camps, it'll end in walls, you watch, and it won't be my people who build them, Grace, it'll be yours. It's already happening, in your well-meaning ways.'

Before

The queues had gone by the time he went up the road to vote. He wouldn't have gone at all but wanted to give the impression that everything was all right, that he was holding it all together.

'They was queuing up to vote this afternoon, Cairo,' his dad said to him, more cheerful than he'd been for years. 'I've never seen nothing like it. Queuing out the door.'

He had work the following morning. It had been patchy since they finished up at the abattoir but Tony wanted him and Alan to go and unload a lorry at a yard in Wednesbury. He was getting picked up at Burnt Tree at seven, that suited him fine. He tried not to think about anything at all.

In the polling booth he looked at the paper, closed his hands into fists, thought he might go there in the booth, lose it, pictured lifting the flimsy partitions, slinging them across the room. He wished he had a lighter, would have set it under the paper, stuck the burning paper in the box, see what they all might do, the officials sitting with their knees squashed under the schoolroom tables. The smell of the school had never changed all these years. He looked at the ballot paper, made his X, folded the paper carefully, put it in the box and left. He could breathe more easily outside. There was music coming from the flats, a dog barked and someone shouted. He thought about all the bones that filled the hill. The helicopter was up already, earlier than was usual, chasing miscreants.

After

He sees her and tells himself that it isn't her, but knows that it is all the same. She sees him at the same time, it seems, or doesn't see him but somehow senses him, looks blindly towards the pub steps, where she saw the men and where she now sees him come round the corner. She had worried about this moment and now it is here.

'Grace.' She has forgotten about Franco, who has gone a dozen steps up the road ahead of her. 'Grace,' he says, and it is Franco's voice, she realizes, startled, as she looks at Cairo and Cairo raises his arm and seems to say her name.

He waves to her. He looks at his hand raised in front of him. He is not usually a man for waving in the street, without a care in the world, it looks. He lets his hand fall to his side and walks towards her.

'Give me a few minutes, Franco,' she says, her throat gone dry, doesn't look at Franco at all, hears him swear under his breath, this petulant boy, thirty years old, and she keeps watching Cairo as he steps out into the road to cross to her. She does not know what she is going to say. And yet she knows suddenly – really knows, not simply knowing things from what people have told her, second-hand knowledge, abstract, the kind of knowledge of which he is so suspicious – that there really are moments on which your life turns.

'Grace,' he says again, and his face is open. The rage is gone and she almost tells him right there, for a second she thinks that he will step up the kerb, and she towards him, and into each other's arms.

He looks at her, the glow of her skin, the light in her eyes, and he wants to touch her, reaches out to her jacket sleeve, holds it gently between his fingers, would like to touch her face, her hair.

'I day think I'd see you again, Grace.' His voice is quiet, she can barely catch what he says, although he looks straight at her. They see themselves in each other's eyes.

'Come to finish the filming, finish everything up,' she says. There are tears at the corners of her eyes, he can see. 'I got that funding, backing, you know, so I need to finish it.'

He nods at this.

'Back where we started, eh?' he says.

But they aren't. And she knows she is not going to tell him, and it shocks her, the way the realization comes suddenly, as if there is a fissure opening between them, the ground opening and the two of them on opposite banks.

'And you?' he says. 'Everything, you all right, you know. Everything gone all right for yer?'

She nods, will not cry. Is uncertain again, that sense of the ground shifting. When she can, she says, 'Everything's OK, yeah, everything went fine, everything's going fine.'

He nods and looks down, glances up the street, looks down again. She feels briefly afraid.

'Look, do you want to get a drink or something,' he says, 'or a cup of tea?'

She can see the light going out in his eyes.

'I tried to phone you,' she says.

'I broke my phone.'

'A last bit of filming. The marketplace, you know. Then I'm done. I'm on the train back in a little while.'

'Well,' he says, 'you take care of yourself, Grace. You take care.'

'Goodbye, Cairo.' She kisses his cheek, gives his hands a squeeze.

And he walks back across the road, turning this time at the dark entrance to the pub.

She places one foot in front of the other. A little over an hour and a half to her train, and you need to allow time for a taxi and the traffic, the station not in the town it says it is, and she'll let Franco take a few shots in the marketplace and back up towards the castle, not talk to anyone, not even try. She tells herself she is not a cruel person, not really. She expects a great flood of tears to come, great aching sobs, but nothing comes. She might have told him. Thinks too late that she might have made a mistake.

*

In the pub he stands at the bar, away from Alan and the others at the table, swallows a pint and orders another, fumbles with the money in his pocket, not much, not much to stay out with. He wonders where the others who sit there have got the money to do this with, he might go for these fuckers here, wants to ask them why they are laughing.

He sees Alan looking across, walk over to him.

'Come and sit down mate, eh?' Alan holds Cairo's arm and Cairo swings his elbow in a wide arc so Alan steps back, his hands up in front of him. 'All right, mate, all right, take it easy. Do whatever you want. Come over when yome ready. All right, all right.'

Alan walks backwards, keeping his good eye on Cairo, who stares back at him and then turns to look at his pint on the bar, sees it off. He hears them call after him but he is away and down the steps and knows what he is going to do, can see himself, as if from a great distance. It happened sometimes, happens more and more these days, like there is the person who acts and the person who looks on, and they are both him, but not the same, like something cleaved in two.

Alan stands on the pub steps and smokes a cigarette. You are meant to go around the back to smoke, away from the door, but who is going to tell him otherwise? He shakes his head. Cairo is better off away from them, although God knows where he's off to now, God knows what's up with him.

He's back in his seat when the woman walks in. He knows who she is, the woman who interviewed Cairo, put him on the telly, one more thing to mess up his head.

'Excuse me,' she says, breathless.

Everything in the barroom has stopped. The men at the table all look at her.

'Excuse me,' she says, tries to smile, looks on the edge of some kind of panic, unmoored. 'You work with Cairo Jukes, I think. Is it Alan?'

He is surprised to hear his own name, that this woman would somehow know it. What Cairo has got himself involved with here, he can only guess at.

'He was here, love, but now he's gone.'

'Do you know where?'

'I ay got a clue,' Alan says, looks at the woman, leans on the legs of his chair, tries to weigh things up and can't. 'He looked about as good as you do, though, but I couldn't tell yer where he's gone, or what he's up to. Have yer phoned him?'

'His phone's bost,' one of the men says.

'Not still?' Alan says, shakes his head.

'If you see him, can you tell him Grace came to look for him.'

'I'd be delighted to, yeah,' he says. 'Grace.'

She turns for the door, eyes following her, she will go to his house, his parents' house. She hears the sound of the men laughing back in the pub. Ann, she thinks, the girl Ann, she has her number, she will ring her, doesn't know why she didn't do this before, why the indecision, the not wanting him to know.

The deal is that Luke leaves the car key under a flowerpot inside his unlocked back gate. The kids don't steal cars any more, not like when they were kids. Maybe they steal better cars than this one. The system works anyway. When he starts the car, Cairo remembers to reach for the glove compartment. There are a couple of lighters in there, half a pack of Mayfair cigarettes.

He nearly simply walked home, lay on his bed, waited for sleep and for Saturday and for Stacey-Ann and Zachariah to come to the door. Cairo has nearly done many things in his life. And now this. He wants them to still be filming. They want a show and he will give them one. The petrol can moves and clangs in the boot, along with the tools and the rags and the last bits of iron, the detritus of the world he is from, and he reverses and turns into the Friday traffic.

The old man, for that is exactly what he is these days, shuffles towards the table in his carpet slippers and says Dudley into the receiver when he answers the phone, says the string of numbers. No one answers the phone like that any more, he supposes, and the voice on the other end of the line speaks over him anyway.

'Grandad, iss Stacey-Ann. Is me dad there?' The girl sounds out of breath, could not have been back at her mother's for more than five minutes and, please God, no more upset.

'I doh know, Stacey-Ann, I doh. Let me have a look? Bear with me. Everything all right, bab?'

'I'm OK, Grandad, all OK. Iss just somebody's trying to get hold of me dad and it's urgent, I think.'

'But yome all right, love? And the babby?'

'Everything's all right, Grandad. Can yer just get me dad?'

He can hear the tension in her voice, everything a drama, all your feelings out in the open all the while, it's what the world has become like. He used to think Cairo was like it, had got like it. And that girl Natalie, terrible, the drama, the ups and downs. Stacey-Ann had got it from her mother, that was for sure. Anybody wants to get hold of you urgently, then it's always bad news. It had happened to them once, years ago, before they had Cairo, they'd gone on holiday to Weston, one of the big hotels along the front, they were on their way out of the evening meal, past the polished dance floor, when a voice had called from reception, 'Mr Jukes?'

There was an urgent message to phone home. His mother had been hit by a bus reversing in Dudley bus station, not even a bus station then, the sloping ground between the Empire Tavern and the Birdcage, under the castle, where there had once been cramped terraces and that had become the hillside bus terminus. So stupid they hadn't flattened the ground out, or found somewhere else for the buses, and coaches, coaches too, it was where they'd got the bloody coach to Weston from, and that is what had killed his mother. She'd been on the way to visit her sister in the Dudley Guest Hospital. Her shopping bag had been open and potatoes went rolling down the hill when the bus hit her, crushed her against another bus long enough to kill her, and he could never understand why she had bought the potatoes first and then gone for the bus and why she couldn't have bought them on the way back and that would probably have saved her life, because she'd have got on the earlier bus, or would have walked without the potatoes to drag her down, or at least wouldn't have been trying to cross between the buses when she did. That is how life comes and goes, he thinks.

'Who is it?' Joan sits in the chair by the kitchen door. He'd been meaning to ask Cairo to set a phone up on the table there, so she wouldn't have to move to answer it when he wasn't there.

'Iss our Stacey-Ann, wants her dad.'

Joan tuts. 'Her ay been gone five minutes. Shouldn't have left in the first place. Probably summat her's done now.' She has referred to Natalie as *her*, as *she*, for all the years she and Cairo have been separated, even during some of the time before they split. 'I bet her's locked her out again, changed her mind.'

'Is he out the back?'

The door is on the latch, he notices. The breeze lifts the net curtain. He stands on the path for a moment. All quiet. The murmur of pigeons and the sound of the leaves in the trees, which always makes him think of the sea. There is the sound of the traffic from the New Road. It is not even called the New Road there, although it is what he has always called it and he has lived here all his life, and he is struck for a moment regarding who owns the names of things. There are the names that appear on maps and signs and there are the names the people use and they are not always the same at all. The traffic, too, has a tidal murmur to it, like waves breaking on a beach, a constancy, something you might normally only notice through its absence. The sound came and went in the afternoon lull.

'Cairo?' he says towards the half-propped-up fence. He'd meant to get Cairo to pour some concrete into that fence post, was fed up of waiting for the council to come and tidy things up, and you'd think that Cairo might think of that for himself, but he still seemed sometimes lost in a dream. 'Cairo?' And he says Cairo again and shivers even though it is warm now, out of the breeze, the sun shines and the clouds are high in the sky.

'No sign of him?' Joan says, when he comes back through the door.

'No,' he says. 'I'll check upstairs.'

'I doh think he's upstairs. Must have gone out again. Cor her phone his mobile?'

'Iss bost, I think,' he says, through the room, the phone already half to his ear, and he can hear Stacey-Ann saying something to the babby.

'That boy,' Joan says. 'I never did know what was going on with him.'

'Yer'll have to write down a message for him, Grandad.'

'Hang on a sec, chick. I'll get a pen out of the drawer.'

He should write it down. He remembers he should have told Cairo that Jamie Iqbal had phoned. It was about him fighting again. That idea was best forgotten.

'Or just remember it. Tell him Grace wants to speak to him, iss important. I'll phone yer back later.'

'Grace?'

'Grace.'

'Who's Grace?'

'It doh matter, Grandad.'

'That nice girl who's doing the film?' he says.

'That one, yeah. Just remember to tell him when he comes in. And tell him I'm sorry.'

'All right, love. Doh worry, I'll remember. I'll tell him.' He can hear the baby crying for a moment before the line goes dead. Always a drama, always a fuss about not much at all, as if the world was not hard enough.

Cairo drives along the side of the stalls, with the stall-holders watching him, some of them packing up now, and a couple of vans parked at angles to load up, and this is probably why no one stops him. A bloke carrying a rail of white underclothes waves at him, points at the car and back down the High Street, says something that Cairo doesn't catch, and no one else tries to stop him. He has his head low over the wheel looking for any sign of them, sees the lad with the camera strutting about near the entrance to the precinct, considers putting his foot down and driving right into him, of doing things that way, then pulls up, the car aslant to the last of the stalls, jumps out and doesn't even shut the door, leaves the keys in the ignition, moves quickly to open the boot.

'What yer doing? Yer cor park there, mate,' a woman shouts from her mobility scooter, and he keeps his head down, pulls at the tarpaulin, the can of petrol, wonders if that is enough.

Tony is cleaning the grooves of his golf clubs and the cleats of his shoes with a tee and an old rag, sitting out on the patio.

'Am yer stopping in for a bit?' she asks him, and she realizes she no longer says dad or Tony, wonders how this will work in the future.

'I am love, yeah. Friday afternoon,' he says, shrugs his shoulders. 'Work's a bit slow, if I'm honest.'

'I wondered if yer could have Zach for half an hour? I've got to pop out, urgent, up Dudley, like.'

'You all right, love? You look like you've seen a ghost.'

'No, I'm all right. I'm all right.'

Stacey-Ann waves him away, runs her hand across the top of the barbecue, moves back towards the patio doors.

'I've changed him. His bottle's on the side there if he starts to cry. I wouldn't normally, you know, but summat's come up.'

'It's OK, love. I'll do it, no problem.'

Zach lies on his mat, laughing at the animal shapes on the mobile she unscrewed from his cot before she left.

'Is it Duane?' he asks.

She is struck by how he says this. No one else uses his name, this absent boy, man, father.

'No,' she says, 'it's me dad.'

She pulls on her sandals, pulls the strap so hard that it breaks, tries not to show it.

'Oh, Stace,' Tony says. 'You watch what yome doing. It's nice to have you back,' he adds, to the percussive slap-slap of her sandals across the tiled floor. 'He looked all right this morning,' he then says, about no one in particular – Cairo, Duane, both of them, he supposes.

Cairo has the kindling gathered in the tarpaulin and shuffles with it away from the car towards the fountain. There are people looking at him now, and surely people he might recognize, who might recognize him and shout, 'All right, Cairo?' Which could snap him out of it, or to which he might reply, 'No, not really. What's it look like to you?' or more likely just say, 'All right, mate,' put his thumb up even, and then go home.

But he doesn't see people he knows, only people he doesn't know shuffle past, veering out of his way, he can see them, apart from a couple of kids in tracksuits standing around a solitary floored bike and smoking a ragged spliff, who nod at him as he goes past like he is some lost pilgrim deserving of a kind of awe. He recognizes one of the boys as the kid from Lupin Road.

They watch Cairo as he continues past the market stalls, lays the tarpaulin on the floor, kneels.

Cairo imagines someone will stop him now, by the fountain, when he drops to his knees, tips the can so that the petrol splashes on the wood and firelighters scattered around him, gives it all a good dousing. There are a couple of men wearing high-visibility coats somewhere off down the line of stalls, security guards, he can see. He imagines them strolling across, the crackle of a walkie-talkie, the nervous glance and decision about whether to approach him. But nothing. A pigeon comes to have a peck at a firelighter and he waves his hand out towards it and it hops a few feet away, not perturbed enough to fly.

He kneels on the wood and the smell of petrol hits him. Something moves in him now, some fear. Someone will stop him. But they want a show. Grace. The sun feels warm, accentuates the smell of the petrol. It has turned into a pleasant day. There is a small crowd gathered near the top of the arcade. It is not for him. He can see the man with the camera, he cannot see Grace.

He lays the rags around him that had been gathered by the petrol can, wasting time. Someone will stop him, save him from himself. He splashes the petrol all around. The pigeon pecks at a splash. He thinks of St Kenelm, the story of the dove that flew from his wound and off to Rome, and wonders where this pigeon might fly, its wings ablaze, what message it might carry, other than that of a burning body. He pours the petrol carefully into the well of his hand, like a lotion, he cups it to his face and fights the sting of it, rubs it through his hair and massages it up his arms, tips the last of it into his lap. Ablutions, they are called, these motions, cleansing. The mosque will be full, Friday afternoon. He thinks of the ritual of the corner, how his dad would hold the bottle to his lips, tighten the laces in his gloves, wipe his Vaselined thumbs under Cairo's eyes. He never cut, barely ever, and if he did the blood would come slow and they could stem it and hide it. Cuts were never a problem. Getting hit was never a problem. They voted to relight the fires. He will be the furnace and the flames.

Franco is filming down the row of shops. Grace sees Cairo at the end of the market stalls. She holds her phone in her hand like a charm. The girl had said she'd come straight here, to wait here. Cairo pulls old shirts from a bag, looks for a moment like a magician performing that trick where the material goes on for ever. Except he has stopped with the material now and has a can in his hands, pours something from it, people moving towards him. And she walks towards him too, and now she runs, because she can see what he is going to do, it is registering in her all the time she moves towards him. She knows what he is going to do, but at the same time cannot know, and his hand shakes, she can see that.

He sits cross-legged among his rags. He fumbles in his pocket for the lighter, puts his lips to the can, feels the sear of the petrol on his face. He hears a voice. Things speed up. The men in the high-vis coats move towards him. There is a woman holding a phone in the air, pointing it towards him. The man filming still has his back turned. The show is here, you wanted a show and here it is. His hands shake as he fumbles with the lighter, and he wonders if it has run out of gas, and he expects to feel hands upon him, because there are people now, moving towards him, and he can hear someone shouting.

'No,' he hears, but it feels very far away, because he is scrabbling with his thumb, clicking the lighter in front of him and he cannot get the flame to catch and then it does and for a moment there is a small blue flame and nothing happens, and then there is a sudden rush of fire and he is alight.

'Cairo,' he hears, 'Cairo,' and he sees her appear through the people moving in front of him, some coming forward, some running away, in a way they always seemed to when he was on the ropes in the ring and you could make out the faces in the front few rows – shouting or laughing or gleeful or scared – and it was like you were somewhere else altogether, miles away. And for a second it doesn't feel like anything, though he can see his hands and arms on fire in front of him, and then he is inside it all, a man on fire. And she is there, for a moment, Grace, and then she is gone.

Someone holds his hand. It is her, Grace, here in the darkness. He can hear voices, quiet, a murmur, and the sound of machines, rhythmic and slow, as if on an aeroplane. And perhaps that is it, they are flying. And she squeezes his hand, says everything is all right, and here they go, and they are flying, he feels them veer away so the earth is there before them and it is a field of lights.

Someone holds her hand. It is him. She feels they are somewhere deep underground. He spoke of caverns, she remembers, of halls so big they sailed barges into them, choirs sang. She can hear voices that swell in this cave far below the surface, an underground babel. She does not know what the voices say and listens hard but cannot make out the words, mournful and joyful, not one word, only the sound of them as shadows flicker on the walls. There is a sudden well of light and the patterns of bones of creatures dead for millions of years. They move through the tunnels and the dark.

From the marketplace comes the glow of candles. Police tape cordons off small fields of darkness. People stand with lit phones, not quite sure what to do. Crowds gather. There are flowers and flags of different territories laid on this first night. Smoke rises from the candles. Hunched figures stand and guard the darkness. People are told gently to go home, ignore the request, and no one is quite sure what to do. The numbers build, the flowers, the candles, the cards, the flags, the people. To be here, just to be here, is what people answer when asked why they are here at all.

THANK YOU

The publisher and the author would like to thank everyone who responded to the Kickstarter funding call for this project. Without your generous support this book would not have been possible.

The author would also like to thank the following people:
Many thanks to Meike Ziervogel, James Tookey and everyone involved with Peirene Press in making this book and the Peirene Now! series happen. To Jacob Polley, for suggesting this collaboration. Thanks also to Hannah Westland and Nick Sheerin at Serpent's Tail, and Sam Copeland at Rogers, Coleridge and White. The character of Cairo Jukes developed in part after separate conversations with Isabella Ferretti, Rob Williams and Phil O'Brien: my gratitude to you. And thank you, as always, to my family for their ongoing support.

Peirene

Contemporary
European Literature.
Thought provoking,
well designed, short.

'*Two-hour books to be
devoured in a single sitting:
literary cinema for those
fatigued by film.*' TLS

Online Bookshop
Subscriptions
Literary Salons
Reading Guides
Publisher's Blog

www.peirenepress.com

Follow us on twitter and Facebook @PeirenePress
Peirene Press is building a community of passionate readers.
We love to hear your comments and ideas.
Please email the publisher at: meike.ziervogel@peirenepress.com

Subscribe

Peirene Press publishes series of world-class contemporary novellas. An annual subscription consists of three books chosen from across the world connected by a single theme.

The books will be sent out in December (in time for Christmas), May and September. Any title in the series already in print when you order will be posted immediately.

The perfect way for book lovers to collect all the Peirene titles.

> *'A class act.'* GUARDIAN

> *'Two-hour books to be devoured in a single sitting: literary cinema for those fatigued by film.'* TLS

£35 1 Year Subscription (3 books, free p&p)

£65 2 Year Subscription (6 books, free p&p)

£90 3 Year Subscription (9 books, free p&p)

Peirene Press, 17 Cheverton Road, London N19 3BB
T 020 7686 1941
E subscriptions@peirenepress.com

www.peirenepress.com/shop
with secure online ordering facility

COUNTERPOINTS ARTS

Peirene Press is proud to support
Counterpoints Arts.

Counterpoints Arts is a charity that promotes the
creative arts by and about refugees and migrants
in the UK.

*'We are living in a time of human
displacement. We need bold and
imaginative interventions to help
us make sense of migration. And
who better to do this than artists
who are engaging with this issue.'*

ALMIR KOLDZIC AND ÁINE O'BRIEN, DIRECTORS, COUNTERPOINTS ARTS

By buying this book you are helping
Counterpoints Arts enhance the cultural
integration of refugees – a mission which will
surely change our society for the better.

Peirene will donate 50p from the sale of this
book to the charity.

www.counterpointsarts.org.uk